MURDER ON
GRE

MARTHA MILLER COSY MYSTERIES – BOOK 4

CATHERINE COLES

B

Boldwood

First published in Great Britain in 2026 by Boldwood Books Ltd.

Cover Design by JD Smith Design Ltd.

Cover Images: Shutterstock

A CIP catalogue record for this book is available from the British Library.

Paperback ISBN 978-1-80415-091-7

Large Print ISBN 978-1-80415-092-4

Hardback ISBN 978-1-80415-090-0

Trade Paperback ISBN 978-1-80656-185-8

Ebook ISBN 978-1-80415-094-8

Kindle ISBN 978-1-80415-093-1

Audio CD ISBN 978-1-80415-085-6

MP3 CD ISBN 978-1-80415-086-3

Digital audio download ISBN 978-1-80415-087-0

This book is printed on certified sustainable paper. Boldwood Books is dedicated to putting sustainability at the heart of our business. For more information please visit https://www.boldwoodbooks.com/about-us/sustainability/

Boldwood Books Ltd, 23 Bowerdean Street, London, SW6 3TN

www.boldwoodbooks.com

For my grandson, Levi John –
May your days be filled with peace, strength, and the quiet joy of knowing you are deeply loved.

Beloved, I wish above all things that thou mayest prosper and be in health, even as thy soul prospereth.

— (3 JOHN 1:2)

CHARACTER LIST

Martha Miller – Protagonist
Stan Miller – Martha's husband
Ruby Andrews – Martha's sister
Luke Walker – Westleham's vicar
Ben Robertson – Police detective inspector
Maud Burnett – Martha's neighbour, loves to repeat gossip
Ada Garrett – Village gossip
Gertrude Felton – Luke's housekeeper
John Bennington – Local farmer
Frank Bennington – John's son
PC Cyril Bottomley – Village policeman
Clifford Baker – Owner of grocer's/post office
Joe & Winnie Noble – Owners of village pub, the Cricketer's Arms
Iris Walker – Luke's sister
Dr Briggs – Village GP
Annie Raynor – Winteringham villager
Ted Harland – Stan's friend from Brighton, accountant
Bernard Harland – Ted's brother, pharmacist
Walter Preston – Local businessman
Oliver Beckwith – Local solicitor
Lavinia Thompson – Winteringham villager
Detective Inspector Kennington – Police detective inspector

1

WESTLEHAM, BERKSHIRE – MAY 1948

I stared out of the window as I washed the breakfast dishes. The sun was high in the sky, and I hoped the spring sunshine would last for the next couple of weekends, at least. While spring showers were good for my garden, I had two far more important reasons for hoping the weather stayed fine.

This coming Saturday was the long-awaited cricket match between Westleham's recently resurrected cricket team and that of the nearby village of Winteringham. I had organised the game with my good friend, Annie Raynor. We had spent way too many hours working out the arrangements for anything to go wrong. I liked to think that not even the weather would dare defy us.

More importantly, the following Saturday was the wedding of my sister Ruby and her beau, Detective Inspector Robertson. After the ceremony, Ruby and Ben would make their home in Westleham. Ben had rented the cottage on the edge of the village which was aptly named Village Edge. I was delighted that Ruby would live nearby..

Village Edge had once been rented by Margaret Leaming, the former secretary of the village committee, and later by the village vicar's father, Vincent Walker. Neither occupant had stayed in the cottage for very long because of their poor character. Ben was not superstitious, so didn't hold with any ideas that the cottage was bad luck. He was more than happy to take the cottage and begin married life there with Ruby.

My sister, on the other hand, was less enthusiastic. She thought the cottage was cursed, and this was rather a bone of contention between the young couple. I couldn't disagree with Ruby, as I wouldn't want to live there myself.

This train of thought brought me back to my own dilemma. My husband, Stan, had left for work in the city nearly two years ago and had never returned. Ruby had come to live with me shortly thereafter, and the money she paid to stay in the spare room, together with our combined ration allowance, ensured I could carry on putting food on the table. Now I wasn't sure how I would manage without Ruby's board.

As usual, thoughts of my marital status brought my feelings around to the village vicar, Luke Walker. I couldn't help but allow a small smile to caress my lips any time I thought of him. The feelings between us had grown since he had arrived in the village; though, of course, we could not and would not act on anything because I was still a married woman.

Luke had promised to go to Village Edge with Ruby before her wedding and bless the cottage. He was of rather the same mindset as Ben and did not believe that houses were the source of bad luck, but he was willing to do whatever he could to relieve Ruby's concerns – especially with the wedding so close.

Maud Burnett, my neighbour, also thought Ruby and I were quite mad. She had told us that old Mrs Finnegan had lived in that cottage for 'nigh on fifty years' with no mishaps. Quite correctly, she also pointed out that Ruby should be glad that Ben had not wanted their first home to be in the middle of London –

which he could well have insisted on, given that that was where his job was based.

Maud had shuddered as she pointed out that there couldn't be many things worse than living in the centre of London, particularly after the bombings. Pointing out that it was probably quite safe to live in London, given that the bombings had ceased some years ago, did not ease Maud's concerns. To her, our nation's capital was a den of iniquity, and there was nothing that could persuade her to travel there for any reason.

When I'd finished in the kitchen, I intended to put on a light jacket and take my dog, Lizzy, for a walk. She was a beautiful Irish Setter and loved meeting people in the village. There had been a time not so long ago when I would have put my head down as I left my house and walked towards Farmer Bennington's field to avoid villagers – I was so embarrassed by Stan's desertion. These days I was happy to meet with my neighbours and talk with them while they stroked Lizzy's proud head or tickled her under the chin.

A knock sounded from the front door, jolting me out of my reverie. Lizzy gave an answering bark. I looked at the clock as though that could tell me who might be at my door. Ordinarily, in our little village, I supposed it probably could. Everything happened at a particular time – from the milkman who did his rounds to the postman delivering letters. I could think of nobody who would call on a Friday at just after nine in the morning though.

Wiping my hands on the dish towel, I walked to the front door. Ruby would have paused at the hall mirror to pat her hair and probably apply a little extra lipstick. I did not. My intention was to take Lizzy for a walk and by the time I returned, my hair would be windblown, and my lipstick non-existent, so it really didn't matter to me what I looked like before I left.

I fixed a smile on my face before I opened the door because I had learned that this was the best way to greet visitors. No longer did I answer my door or enter rooms with my head down because I was humiliated that my husband had left me, or worried that I would have nothing to say that would interest anyone.

The warmth of my smile faded, leaving only the bewilderment of shock as I saw who was standing on my doorstep.

Standing there, as if nearly two years hadn't passed, was my errant husband, Stan.

* * *

Looking at the door that still stood between us, I made a conscious effort to close my mouth. 'Do you want to come in?'

The question was automatic, and I regretted the words as soon as I said them. Stan blinked. 'I wasn't sure of my welcome.'

'This is still your house,' I replied, a slight note of accusation in my voice while I desperately tried to maintain both my dignity and temper. After all, it would do no good to have a shouting match – especially on the doorstep. What was done was done, as Maud would say. I stood back and held the door wide so that he could come in.

Lizzy danced around his feet for a few moments before she seemed to remember who he was. Stan had never been unkind to Lizzy, but he had never taken to her. It was fair to say that they tolerated each other and no more.

'How have you been?' he asked as I led the way through to the kitchen. Visitors were usually shown into the parlour. If they asked for a drink, I would go into the kitchen and prepare one – I would never ordinarily take guests into the kitchen.

Stan was not a visitor.

Neither was he a guest.

He was… My stomach flip-flopped like a fish out of water.

This man was my husband – the one I had promised to love until death parted us.

The realisation of what his reappearance would mean for me hit me with more force than I used when beating dust out of my rugs. It had taken me a long time to come to terms with being deserted. I was a married woman, yet somehow single, too. A woman who had a spouse but somehow was free to make her own decisions and who was responsible for her own choices. In recent times, I had embraced that version of myself.

My palms were damp, and I picked up the dishcloth from next to the sink and absently wiped my hands. 'Can I get you a cup of tea? I think there's some left in the pot. I can soon refresh it.'

It was 'real tea' and not the lavender tea I preferred. Ruby and I always had ordinary tea in the morning before she left for work.

'That would be nice,' Stan said, though his expression was doubtful.

He took a seat at the table, and I tried not to resent that he had done so without me offering him the chair. I was making a big effort to act normally – he was probably just doing the same. And, after all, as I'd told him moments earlier, this was his house.

I had struggled to pay money into the bank to pay the housing costs, but I had done it. Mostly because of the money Ruby had paid for her room. Money which I was about to lose. Dread filled me as I wondered about the reason for his return.

Was he going to sell the house?

Perhaps he had come to ask me for a divorce?

Or could the reason for his return be worse? Did he intend to come back and resume our marriage as though the last few years had not happened?

I didn't know which of those things was worse.

Blindly, with tears filling my eyes, I stumbled over to the stove to put the kettle on to boil so I could refresh the teapot.

Blinking to clear my vision, I looked again at the clock. Quarter past nine. It was too late for breakfast, and too early for lunch. What does a wife offer a husband who has been missing for over two years on his return?

'Can I—' I started and swallowed. 'Is there anything else I can get you?'

'No.' He looked at me for what felt like the first time in forever. I waited for his appraisal to be over. I had never felt like I was quite enough for Stan. The belief that I was distinctly lacking flooded through me once more.

Whether it was the meals I served, the way I kept his home, which obviously was not as good as the way his mother had done it, or the more personal parts of our relationship – I had always been aware I was not what he wanted.

Even with my limited knowledge on such things, I knew that a husband and wife having separate rooms from the night that they were married was not usual. Even more unusual were the infrequent times he visited my room. The complete experience of marriage had left me feeling empty, insecure, and wishing I had stayed home to help my mother with my younger siblings instead.

Attempting to be a grown-up by leaving home and getting married had not been at all what I thought it would be. More confusing to me was why Stan had even got married when he clearly didn't seem to want a wife. Unless, of course, it was just me that he didn't want. Perhaps there had been another woman in his life he wanted and could not have, and so he'd simply settled for me.

He gestured towards the kettle at the same time as the

whistling that announced it was boiling burst through my thoughts.

I nodded as though he'd spoken, hating that I was still desperately keen, despite everything, to please Stan. 'Yes, yes, of course. Just one moment and I'll get you your tea.'

'I don't really care about tea, Martha,' he said.

I struggled not to let his words bother me. Of course he didn't want tea. He never wanted anything that I offered. Hadn't I always said and done the wrong thing? I grabbed the kettle, put it down on the iron trivet in the middle of the table, and sat down heavily in the chair opposite Stan, questions swirling in my brain.

I wanted to know where he'd been and why he'd been away for so long, but most of all, why he'd come back now. Why wasn't I asking these questions? Why was I sitting there as meek as I'd been during our marriage, waiting for him to say whatever it was he'd come to say? I wasn't that same woman any more, was I? I had hoped that I was different now. Goodness knows I'd had to be.

My thoughts crashed into each other. Not once had I wondered who he had been with. That said more about our marriage than perhaps even his disappearance did. I always wondered where Luke was and who he had been visiting. I dreaded the day an attractive single woman came to the village, and he realised life was short and he no longer wanted to wait for me to be free so he could have the family I knew he craved.

'You must be wondering why I'm here,' he said, as though he could read my mind.

I folded my arms, Maud-style, and a little of her no-nonsense vigour trickled through me. 'That thought had crossed my mind.'

'You're angry.' He gave a couple of sharp nods. 'I don't blame you, Martha. I've behaved very badly towards you, and for that, I sincerely apologise.'

Opening my mouth to respond, I closed it again. Stan had apologised. He never did that. Not only had he done so, but it sounded very sincere. Was it possible that I wasn't the only one who had changed? Try as I might, I couldn't find fault with his words or his delivery. He meant what he had said.

Unable to think of anything clever to say, I simply said, 'Yes, you have.'

'I read about your sister getting married in the newspaper.'

'Did you?' I asked, dumbfounded. Of all the things I expected him to say, my sister's nuptials were not on the list.

'Your parents put an announcement in the newspaper,' he said, as though that cleared up any confusion. 'It said that she was getting married here in Westleham, and, well, it made me think of our wedding.'

My stomach felt queasy. The small breakfast I'd had earlier swished about uncomfortably with the tea I'd washed it down with.

Stan had thought about our wedding.

Did that mean he regretted leaving me, our marriage, and our home?

Luke's face filled my mind. We both knew that our relationship was not entirely proper. We had tried so hard to only be friends, but our feelings were too strong. However, we worked hard so that we didn't cross the invisible line that society had drawn between us.

Luke had confessed that he loved me, and I loved him. I loved Luke the way that a wife should love a husband. I loved him the way I had never loved Stan.

'We made lifelong promises to each other that day.' I forced the words past my tight throat.

'We never should have got married,' he said abruptly. Although those were the words that I had thought many times before and several times that morning, they still stung. I looked down at the table because somehow looking into his face while he spoke these honest words to me was too much to bear. 'I'm sorry, Martha. I'm sure that must sound very cruel, but I certainly don't mean it to.'

For a moment, I wanted to cry. I wanted to weep at the sadness of being married to a man who did not want me. I wanted to wail against the unfairness of it all. For if I had simply met Luke before Stan, then we would be married. And I would be happy. Luke would be happy. Perhaps even Stan would be happy.

But we had not. So now Luke and I existed in a world where we stole glances at each other and occasionally let our hands linger on each other for slightly longer than was appropriate. Even those small things felt risqué in our small village where there were always eyes on propriety.

The unfairness of my situation caused the anger I had tamped down earlier to bubble up and erupt from me. 'Yes, it is cruel. Where have you been, and why did you abandon me?'

The back door creaked open, and Maud stuck her head around. 'Oh, you have a visitor.'

I forced myself to smile at my neighbour. After all, it wasn't her I was angry with, though she knew well that I had a visitor before she popped through the gate between our back gardens and into my kitchen. She missed nothing. Not one thing that went on in our village, let alone visitors to my house.

'Good morning, Mrs Burnett,' I said.

'Oh, my goodness.' Maud ignored me and stared at Stan. 'It's you, Mr Miller. You're back.'

The hesitancy in her words was almost unbelievable. Maud

was never usually lost for words. Normally it was the other way around – we had trouble finding a way to stop her talking. Even she was almost stunned into silence by the return of my husband.

'I wonder... um... Mrs—'

'Burnett,' Maud supplied. 'Mrs Maud Burnett. From next door.'

She'd been our neighbour for years, but of course Stan had never bothered to learn her name. Not that I'd had too much to do with her before Stan's disappearance. I'd been trying too hard to make him happy. Gossiping with neighbours was something I knew he wouldn't approve of, and so I had not done it.

After he left, I'd been too ashamed of my stand-offish behaviour and Stan's disappearance to make a friend of Maud. I was so glad that events had conspired to change how I felt and show me how much I needed friends in the village.

'Well, Mrs Burnett,' he said. 'I wonder if you'd mind giving Mrs Miller and myself some time alone?'

Maud looked at me, and I nodded to signify I was all right. Well, not really all right, of course, but that I did not need her to stay. 'I'll come and see you later.'

Maud nodded and, with one last look at Stan, left me alone once more with my husband.

* * *

After Maud left, I lifted the teapot lid, added a little more tea from the canister, then poured hot water on top. Grabbing the sugar and milk from the pantry where I had put them after Ruby left for work, I placed them in the middle of the table. Finally, I put a cup and saucer on the table. Stan would have a cup of tea whether or not he wanted one – I needed to do something other than sit at the table opposite him.

Stan gestured at the crockery. 'Where's your cup, Martha? Are you not having tea? I hope you're not using your precious tea ration on me and going without yourself.'

It was astonishing to me that Stan had even thought of such a thing. 'I've already had two cups this morning.'

Hopefully, that brief explanation would suffice. I certainly didn't want to tell Stan that if I had another cup of tea, I feared it would not stay in my stomach. There were some things that a wife simply didn't share with her husband, and, in any event, it wasn't as though we were the type of couple that shared confidences.

'You have every right to be furious with me,' he said then.

My hands were already shaking, and this Stan in front of me – the contemplative one who seemed to actually think about me and my feelings – was so different from the man that I'd known that I was completely thrown off kilter.

I pointed at the teapot. 'Shall I pour?'

'Martha,' he said, and his voice was incredibly gentle. I had never heard him use that tone of voice before. 'I can pour my own tea.'

Of course I knew that, but despite my anger, I had fallen back into trying to please Stan. I wanted this conversation to be over and for him to leave the house. Stupidly, I wanted him to go so I could try to pretend that his visit had never happened.

'I'm going to tell you where I've been,' he said as he poured milk into the bottom of his teacup.

'All right,' I said uselessly.

'I've been in Brighton with a colleague from the bank. We were friends during the war. I've been living at his house with him and his brother.'

'What have you been doing for work, because I know you didn't return to the bank after you left that day?' The question was mundane, and I wanted to say so much more. 'After you left' didn't really cover it. He had left me, his job, his entire life, and completely disappeared without a word to anyone.

His eyes were downcast as though he was ashamed of his behaviour, but he hadn't sounded regretful when telling me where he had been. 'Ted, the friend I mentioned, has an accountancy firm. I've been working with him.'

The resentment I'd felt these last years when I'd had to scrimp and save every penny while he was living with friends in Brighton working a respectable job threatened to overwhelm me. 'You left me practically penniless.'

'Was the maintenance I sent each month not enough?' Stan looked confused.

'What maintenance?' Exasperation seeped into every word. 'The local bank manager wouldn't tell me anything. He said the account was in your name and the only way he could give me access to it was if you were dead. I had to look through your papers to find out how much the mortgage was and make sure I paid in enough money to cover it.'

He shook his head, clearly bewildered. 'I arranged with Oliver Beckwith for him to send you a postal order every month.'

Oliver Beckwith was the village solicitor. 'I have heard nothing from him.'

Stan looked as though he wanted to hurl his teacup across the room. For all his faults, he had never been an angry or aggressive man. 'I will speak to Beckwith today. I promise you, Martha, I left explicit instructions with him. He's a solicitor, so naturally I trusted him.'

Since he'd been gone, I'd scrimped and saved to make ends meet. Yet now, somehow, I almost felt grateful I hadn't received the money he'd sent. Without it I'd learned to stand on my own two feet, and by taking in my sister as a lodger, I'd gained a close and loving relationship with her. Still, the constant worry and sleepless nights pressed heavily on my chest – all that fear and scraping by, and for what?

'Why now?' I asked with a heavy sigh. 'Why have you come home now?'

'It's like I said.' Stan took a sip of tea, and I recognised the gesture for what it was – he was both stalling and calming his irritation. 'I saw the notice of Ruby's marriage in the newspaper, and I thought about our wedding and the promises I made to you. Most of which I have broken. I thought it was past time I came back to Westleham and organised my affairs properly.'

I wanted to ask him which promises he had broken. Did it include the one where he had promised to remain faithful to me until the day he died? Despite our patently loveless marriage, I didn't want to know the answer to that. I closed my eyes and Luke's face swam through my thoughts.

'Are you coming back?' I asked then, the question that I wanted the answer to most bursting out of me. 'To me, I mean. Are you coming back here to the house to live with me?'

'No,' he said quickly. 'No, I'm not.'

I tried not to show my complete relief. 'I see.'

'I've come to settle things up. It seems not a moment too soon given Beckwith's behaviour. I'm going to sign the house over to you, Martha. That is, I intend to put the house in your name.'

'What about the mortgage?' I asked mechanically.

'I've made some investments,' he said. His obvious happiness was so out of place for both Stan's character and the situation. 'My friend Ted helped me, and I'm pleased to say I have enough money to pay off the mortgage. So that is what I shall do. Then you will own this house, and it will be yours to do with as you wish. You can go wherever you want and do whatever you like. You won't be tied to this village.'

Little did Stan know that I would be tied to Westleham for as long as Luke remained here. However, I nodded, as though his words had been exactly what I had expected. My mind swirled with possibilities and emotions I had no time to process. 'Thank you.'

'It's the very least I can do,' he said, and I did not contradict him. 'I will, of course, continue to send money for your support, though I will have to find out why that hasn't been getting to you in my absence. I don't want you to struggle because of my decisions.'

'Lack of funds is why Ruby came to live with me. I have been struggling, Stan.'

He glanced at me, bit his lip, and then looked away. 'I am so sorry, Martha. I shall never forgive myself for what I did to you, although it was the right thing for me. I realise I must have made your life extremely difficult. It must have been dreadful for you.'

Again, I could not contradict what he said. Every word was correct, but yet, that did not change a thing. Having the house in my name and a sum of money each month on which to live would be extremely useful. Much more than I could have ever hoped for. Yet the crucial thing remained the same – Stan and I were still married. Even if we divorced, I still could not marry Luke because he was a vicar.

Luke had always wanted to be a vicar, and despite being an army chaplain and seeing things during the war that no man should ever have to see, his faith had remained strong.

'Where are you staying?' I asked, glad he had not left his luggage on the doorstep.

'We've taken a room at the pub,' he said. 'I travelled with my friend Ted and his brother Bernard, arriving late last night. We thought we'd stay for the weekend, organise things today, finalise the paperwork on Monday and then travel back to Brighton.'

'Yes, I see,' I said for what felt like the one hundredth time, but I didn't really see anything. 'There's a cricket match tomorrow. You and your friends might enjoy it.'

I don't know why I told him that. Probably because I simply didn't know what else to say. His visit had been such a great shock. He looked at me questioningly. 'A cricket match?'

'Westleham has resurrected its cricket team,' I said. 'Remember, there was one before the war.'

'Not really,' he said, and that did not surprise me. He hadn't integrated into village life at all when he lived in Westleham. Yet I knew he must have played cricket while he was at university as he had whites, gloves, pads, and even a cricket bat in the bottom of his wardrobe.

'Where are your friends now?' I asked.

'At the pub.' Stan cleared his throat. 'I didn't think it would be a good idea for me to bring them here to the house. I thought our conversation needed to be held in private. After all, it's been so long since we've seen each other, I wasn't at all sure of my welcome.'

'Most wives would have slammed the door in your face,' I told him.

'Yes,' he agreed. 'I'm sure they would.'

'Now, have you arranged to take lunch at the pub, or shall I—'

Stan held out a hand and reached across the table and placed it over mine. 'Martha, please stop. Stop trying to please me. You don't have to do that. We are not—'

This time, it was Stan who stopped talking and looked horribly embarrassed. I looked away and Stan removed his hand. He had been about to say we were not married but, of course, we were. People didn't stop being married just because they both wished for it to be so.

'This is rather a mess, isn't it?' I asked with a rueful chuckle.

'Yes,' Stan agreed, and we shared an uncomfortable smile. 'But I promise you I will put things right with Oliver Beckwith and make the arrangements for the transfer of the house and your maintenance before I leave.'

We both looked towards the hallway as another knock sounded at my front door. I looked up again at the clock, as though that would help tell me who was on the other side. I walked down the corridor and opened the door. Luke stood there with a broad smile on his handsome face.

'Martha, is everything all right? You've normally left to walk Lizzy by now, and I happened to notice that you have not come out of your house yet today.' He stopped talking and looked over my shoulder.

Without turning round, I knew Stan had followed me out of the kitchen. I looked at Luke and blinked away the tears that flooded my eyes.

'Good morning, Vicar,' I said then. The false brightness in my voice must have been obvious to both men. 'You haven't met my husband, Stan. Stan, this is Luke Walker, Westleham's village vicar.'

My heart splintered as I introduced Luke as though he meant nothing to me.

2

Luke did not come into the house, and Stan left shortly after Luke's departure. No sooner had I closed the door on Stan than the sound of my back door opening and closing signalled the arrival of Maud. It did not take me long to tell her about Stan's visit.

Although Maud was known as a village gossip, I trusted she would not share my personal affairs with our neighbours. After one of her no-nonsense pep talks, I had worked up enough courage to take Lizzy for her walk. No doubt Stan's return would be the topic of conversation on everyone's lips as they enjoyed their lunch.

I walked past the vicarage, towards the village green, carefully keeping my gaze straight ahead. Bunting flapped in the breeze – a cheerful collection of Union Jacks and faded fabric triangles that had seen better days. However, they signalled a sort of hopefulness; after the terrible years of war, Westleham was finally regaining its joy.

It was one of those spring days that hinted that summer wasn't far off. Lizzy trotted beside me, her russet coat gleaming in the pale sunshine, nose twitching as she investigated every gatepost and tuft of grass. The bunting's gaiety stood in stark contrast to my troubled emotions.

Stan was back. No matter how often I reminded myself of that fact, it still refused to feel real. It hung in the air like the scent of the lavender sachets in my linen cupboard – familiar, cloying, and impossible to ignore.

As I passed by the village green, I saw three men standing by the low stone wall outside Oliver Beckwith's solicitor's office. Two were unfamiliar, though they looked vaguely alike in posture and build. One was tall, with neatly parted hair and the air of someone who thought highly of his own opinions.

The other was broader across the shoulders and stood slightly behind the other two with a quiet watchfulness. The third man I recognised easily because, of course, it was Stan. He saw me before I had a chance to turn away and hurry in the direction of Farmer Bennington's fields.

'Martha,' he called, lifting a hand.

I tightened my grip on Lizzy's lead and forced myself to approach the three men.

'Good morning,' I said, trying to sound brighter than I felt.

'We were trying to get an appointment with Oliver Beckwith, as I told you I would.' Stan gestured to the other two men. 'Let me introduce you. This is the friend I told you about, Edward Harland, and his brother Bernard.'

Ted was the quieter man – the one who had stood behind the other two. He now stepped forward with a polished smile and extended his hand.

'Mrs Miller, it is an absolute pleasure to meet you. Stan has told me so much about you.'

I shook his hand and tried not to look surprised. How interesting that he knew all about me, when I had known absolutely nothing of him until that very day. The accountant's palm was warm and confident with no hint of moisture. Under different circumstances, I felt sure I would quite like Ted. However, he seemed to be a big reason for Stan staying in Brighton and deserting me. It also rankled me that Ted and Bernard had accompanied Stan to the solicitor's office. Surely the business Stan had there was between him and Oliver Beckwith and nothing whatsoever to do with the other two men.

'Goodness,' I said, glancing at Stan. 'I'm surprised to hear that – he has never been much of a talker.'

Ted laughed as though I had made a joke.

Stan cleared his throat. 'We were just saying how nice the village green looks. It's ready for the cricket match you told me about.'

'It does,' I agreed. 'Everyone's been working hard. We're all rather proud of the match tomorrow. The first one since the war.'

Before anyone could reply, the green front door of Beckwith & Co. Solicitors creaked open. Out stepped Oliver Beckwith, his usual pompous air intact as he adjusted his perfectly knotted dark grey tie. His polished shoes clicked against the stone pavement.

'Beckwith!' Stan leaned towards the solicitor, his voice sharper than I'd ever heard it.

Oliver turned, startled. 'Oh! Mr Miller, it's you. I wasn't aware you were back in Westleham.'

'No, I don't imagine you were. I suppose I am the last person you expected to see. I've been trying to get an appointment with you all morning, but your secretary said you were out.'

Oliver raised his chin. 'I had an important engagement. Urgent business.'

'You must have had a lot of that recently.' Stan advanced another step. 'We agreed that you were to send money to Martha every month. I left very clear instructions. I trusted you to carry them out.'

Oliver's nostrils flared. 'If you wish to discuss a private matter, Mr Miller, you should make that appointment you just spoke about. I don't conduct my business in the street.'

'That's a little hard given you never seem to be in your office,' Stan replied. 'Perhaps we can both step back inside and arrange a mutually convenient time?'

Oliver's face flushed. He turned away. 'Good day, Mr Miller.'

'Not so fast!' Stan reached out, grasping Oliver's arm. The solicitor pulled at his arm and in his haste to get away from Stan, he stumbled. With a surprised cry, he toppled over the low stone wall, landing in a heap on the other side.

'Oh, good heavens!' I gasped, rushing forward.

Stan backed away, his hands raised in the air. 'I didn't mean — He lost his balance.'

Ted and Bernard reached the solicitor's side and Bernard knelt beside Oliver.

'Don't touch me!' Oliver barked, wincing. 'It's my ankle. I think it's broken.'

'We should get the doctor,' I said, my heart pounding at the turn of events.

'I'm not a doctor,' Bernard said calmly, 'but I am a pharmacist, and I do have experience in dealing with minor injuries.'

'Bernard worked with the Red Cross a lot during the war,' Ted said to me. 'But perhaps you're right and we should fetch the doctor. Could you direct me?'

I had no sooner given Ted directions to Dr Briggs's house when Maud Burnett reached my side, her eyes wide with curiosity. 'What's happened?'

'Mr Beckwith took a fall,' I said.

'I was pushed,' Oliver retorted as he eyed Stan.

Stan looked horrified. 'It was an accident; you know it was.'

Bernard stood and brushed off his trousers. 'I don't think there's anything broken, but he won't be walking on that leg for the next few days, at least.'

Maud clucked her tongue. 'Well, he certainly won't be playing cricket tomorrow, that's for sure.'

A small crowd had now gathered to see what the fuss was about. Luke strode towards me, his clerical collar stark against his shirt. 'Did I hear that someone is hurt?'

'Only Mr Beckwith's pride,' Maud quipped.

Luke peered over the stone wall. 'Are you all right? Perhaps we could move you to the bench, or maybe inside where you might be a little more comfortable.'

Oliver held up a hand. 'No! Don't move me. I've told you – I'm in an awful lot of pain. I'm staying here until the doctor arrives.'

'Well,' Maud said loudly, 'Mr Miller accosting Mr Beckwith has rather ruined our cricket team tomorrow.'

'You played at university, didn't you, Stan?' I asked innocently, recalling clearly the equipment in the bottom of his wardrobe, together with his dislike of integrating into village life.

As though he could read my mind, Luke turned to Stan. 'Replacing Mr Beckwith in the team seems like the very least you could do.'

Stan stared at Luke, and for a moment, I thought that my husband would refuse. But to my surprise, he summoned up a smile. 'Yes, Vicar. Of course I will take Oliver's place. It will be no trouble.'

* * *

The doctor arrived and quickly dispersed the crowd. With a nod in my direction, Stan, Ted and Bernard headed over the road towards the Cricketer's Arms, where they were staying.

'Don't forget about the game in the morning,' Luke called after them. 'Be at the pavilion for ten. We start at eleven sharp.'

'Yes, Vicar,' Stan called back in an extremely un-Stan-like voice that could only be described as meek.

With a little wave and an extremely inappropriate wink, Maud walked back to her house, leaving Luke to accompany me on my walk.

'I'm meeting Ruby at Village Edge this evening,' Luke said in a rather stilted voice, as though he wanted to talk to me but had no idea how to find a safe subject. 'To bless the house, as she asked.'

'Yes, she told me.'

'I think maybe Oliver's ankle is just sprained.' Luke tried again to find a safe subject.

'Probably.' I hated that I was as awkward as he was. Ordinarily, we had plenty to say to each other and never struggled for conversation. Today, however, had not been an ordinary day.

'It's very hard to keep pretending, Martha,' he said.

I stopped then and turned to look at him. 'What do you mean?'

'You know what I mean,' he said quietly. 'In front of Stan, I have to pretend that you're just another parishioner.'

'Oh, Luke,' I whispered. 'We've been pretending for months now.'

'It's different now Stan is back. You must know that. I can already feel the distance between us. Don't you hate it as much as I do?'

'Yes, I hate it,' I admitted. 'Even more so today, but, Luke, he isn't staying in Westleham. He's going to pay off the mortgage and transfer the house to me. He also said he will ensure I receive money for my support. Apparently I should've been receiving money all these months he's been gone, but for some reason, it hasn't happened.'

'Is that why he wants to see Oliver Beckwith?'

'I suppose so, yes. I don't understand the legalities of it, but I think the solicitor would have to draw up a transfer of the house from Stan's name into mine. But the reason Stan was so cross with Mr Beckwith was because he was the one who was supposed to make sure I received money every month.'

'Oh, I see. How awful. No wonder Stan looked furious.'

'Well, that's just it,' I said. 'Stan tried to make an appointment to discuss all these matters, but Oliver tried to fob him off and walk away. Stan grabbed hold of him and Oliver fell over. It was an accident, but it's so unlike Stan to be so angry. I've never seen him like that before.'

'Do you believe him... about the money?'

'I have no reason not to believe what he says,' I said. 'And he was certainly angry enough to confront Oliver about it.'

'What now?'

I shook my head sadly. 'Nothing will change. I will have a little more money, and I will own a house, but Stan and I will still be married.'

Luke's darkly fringed blue eyes stared into mine. 'He didn't mention divorce?'

'No, he didn't. And we both know it wouldn't matter if he had.'

'Don't you want to be divorced from him?'

'Of course I do.' I looked away from Luke then, from the pain reflected in his eyes. I was afraid if I continued to look into his tortured expression, I would break down and cry. I couldn't do that in the middle of the village.

'Maybe I should—'

'Don't say it.' I held up a hand. 'Don't say it, Luke.'

'But perhaps—'

I walked on a few steps and then turned back. Luke was still standing in the same spot, a deep frown shadowing his handsome face.

'Don't say things you don't mean.'

'But that's just it, Martha.' His voice broke. 'I don't want to leave the Church, but if that's what it will take for us to be together, then that is what I must do.'

He turned away before I could say anything in response to his proclamation. He opened the gate at the top of the path to the vicarage and disappeared from view.

For a few moments, I just stared, unable to believe what he had said. His words were all of my dreams come true, but they had not made me happy. If anything, I was more confused than ever.

3

The sound of Ruby's key turning in the front door that evening was more welcome than any other evening I could remember – even those before I had made friends in Westleham when I had always felt desperately alone. My mind flitted between Stan's return and Luke's shocking declaration.

'Martha?' Ruby's voice carried down the hallway. 'Are you in the kitchen?'

For a moment I smiled, grateful that something hadn't changed. I was always in the kitchen when Ruby returned from work but that didn't matter. She always called out the exact same greeting.

'Yes,' I answered.

Ruby appeared in the doorway, still wearing her navy-blue coat. Her dyed blonde hair was pinned neatly beneath a small hat, her eyes shining with excitement. 'Is it true?'

'Probably,' I said wearily as I put the kettle on to boil. 'What have you heard?'

'Stan's back, he physically assaulted Oliver Beckwith in the street, and the stuffed shirt is telling everyone that will listen that Stan is an absolute maniac and he will have him arrested for grievous bodily harm.'

'It's mostly true.'

Ruby took off her coat and went into the hall to hang it up. When she returned, she sat down at the kitchen table and began pulling out hat pins. 'I think you had better start at the beginning.'

'Do you want to eat now or—'

'I can't eat at a time like this!' Ruby declared dramatically.

'All right. So, as you know, Stan returned this morning.'

Ruby looked up to the ceiling with a wary expression, pointed, and lowered her voice. 'Is he up there?'

I shook my head. 'At the Cricketer's Arms.'

'Thank goodness for that.'

'Among other things, he told me that before he left he arranged with Oliver Beckwith to send a sum of money each month to support me.'

'Which, of course, you have never received. Is that why Stan attacked Mr Beckwith?'

'He didn't attack him.' I got up as the kettle whistled. 'The solicitor tried to walk away while Stan was attempting to get an appointment with him to discuss the missing money, and to transfer the house into my name.'

'What!' Ruby's astonishment made the word sound like an exclamation rather than a question.

'That was my reaction too,' I said as I brought the kettle over and set it on the trivet in the middle of the table. 'Apparently while he's been away, he's made some good investments. Whatever that means. So he intends to pay off the mortgage and put the house into my name.'

Ruby raised an eyebrow. 'Then what will he do?'

'Go back to Brighton with his friends.'

'Stan has friends? Friends plural?'

I smiled at her incredulity. In the five minutes Ruby had been home, she had already brightened my day. 'Apparently so. Ted and Bernard Harland are brothers with whom he has been staying.'

'Gosh.' Ruby rested her chin in her upturned hands. 'How do you feel about all of this, Martha? It must have been a terrible shock.'

'I don't really know what I feel,' I admitted. 'Shocked, certainly. Confused, angry, as well as a little relieved he isn't dead. As you know our marriage wasn't happy, but I hated to think all these months that he had died and I didn't even know.'

Ruby clapped a hand over her mouth. 'What about Luke? How does he feel?'

'He spoke about leaving the Church.' I was so relieved to share that piece of information with someone else.

'Goodness.' Ruby closed her mouth, opened it again, then changed her mind.

'Indeed.' I mechanically spooned tea into the teapot. 'And that might not even be the strangest thing that happened today.'

'Stranger than Stan coming home, attacking the solicitor, and Luke talking of leaving the Church?' Ruby shook her head vehemently. 'Nothing can be odder than those things.'

I stirred the teapot, then replaced the lid to let the tea stew. 'You mustn't say that Stan attacked Mr Beckwith. He didn't. He grabbed his arm, Mr Beckwith then tried to get free, stumbled, and fell over the wall.'

Ruby put a hand over her mouth in a vain attempt to hide a giggle. 'Oh my! What I wouldn't give to have had a ringside seat at that little set-to.'

'You shouldn't laugh,' I said, even as a smile tugged at the corners of my mouth.

'Why not?' Ruby asked as she dropped her hand and laughed out loud. 'Oliver Beckwith is such an old stick in the mud!'

'He is rather,' I agreed as I joined in Ruby's laughter.

When she had calmed, and wiped her eyes, she spooned a teaspoon of sugar into one of the cups I had put out on the table. 'Now, do tell, what is the most peculiar thing that happened today?'

'Stan agreed to play for the village cricket team.'

'Stan? Playing cricket? For the village?' Ruby looked as though I had told her that Lizzy had learned to speak French. 'The same Stan who never bothered to attend the Harvest Festival or the Christmas nativity?'

'I know it seems unlikely, but Luke rather backed him into a corner about it. Said it was the least he could do after causing Oliver's injury.'

Ruby grinned. 'Good old Luke. Tell me, what did you say to Luke when he spoke about leaving the Church?'

'Nothing. I couldn't. He walked away before I could respond. Ruby, what am I to do? I never wanted Luke to sacrifice his calling for me. The Church means everything to him.'

'Is it more important to him than you are?' she asked gently.

'It should be,' I said firmly. 'A vicar's duty is to God first, always. I would never forgive myself if he gave up everything he's worked for, everything he believes in, just because my husband abandoned me.'

'I don't suppose Stan being back changes anything?'

I shook my head sadly and tried not to cry again. 'It doesn't. Nothing will really change, Ruby. I'll still be married to a man I don't love, and who doesn't love me. I'll still be trapped.'

Ruby lifted the lid on the teapot, gave a nod of satisfaction, then replaced it. 'Tea, Martha?'

'I don't think I could manage it, my stomach has been in knots all day.'

She went into the pantry, retrieved a bottle of the plum gin I made myself and got two small glasses. 'Then we shall have a little tipple.'

I glanced at the clock. 'It's very early.'

'It's nearly six o'clock,' she retorted. 'And after the day you've had, I would say that you needed a stiff drink some hours ago.'

She was right. I had gone through so many different emotions that day, I welcomed the plum gin numbing the edges of my sadness. I accepted the glass she filled for me. 'Thank you.'

'You know, when I agreed to marry Ben, I was terrified.'

'Were you?' I was surprised by this admission. Ruby had always seemed so confident about her decision.

'Absolutely terrified. Not of Ben, of course, but of marriage itself. Of promising to love someone forever, of trusting them not to leave.' She gave me a look full of such compassion I wondered for a moment which of us was the older sibling. 'Watching what Stan did to you, and how difficult it has been for you since, made me wonder if any man could be trusted with a woman's heart.'

'What changed your mind?'

'Ben did. Not through grand gestures or pretty words, but through consistency. Day after day, month after month, he showed me that his feelings were real and lasting. That's how I knew I could trust him with my future.' She took a sip of her gin, made a face, then gulped it down. 'Luke has done the same for you, hasn't he? Shown you, through his actions, that his love is genuine?'

'Yes,' I whispered, though I was afraid to admit it to Ruby, let alone myself. 'Even when he couldn't say the words, I could see it in the way he looked at me, the way he worried about me, and even the fuss he makes of Lizzy.'

'Then perhaps you should trust him to know his own mind about the Church.'

'But, Ruby—'

'I'm not saying you should encourage him to leave his calling,' she interrupted gently. 'I'm simply suggesting that you might consider that Luke is a grown man who can make his own decisions about what matters most to him.'

'Goodness,' I said in shock as I blinked away tears. 'When did you get so wise?'

Before Ruby could respond, there was a knock at the front door. Ruby and I looked at each other.

'Are you expecting someone?' she asked.

'No. Though given the day I've had, I suppose it could be anyone.'

* * *

I made my way to the front door, Ruby following behind. When I opened it, I found Ben Robertson and Cyril Bottomley standing on my doorstep. Ben, a detective inspector, was Ruby's fiancé. Cyril was the village policeman. Ben's usually cheerful face wore a serious expression.

'Good evening, Martha. Ruby.' He nodded to both of us. 'I'm sorry to disturb you, but PC Bottomley and I wondered if we might have a word about the incident with Mr Beckwith earlier today?'

'Of course,' I said, stepping back to let them in. I led the way through to the lounge. 'Can I get anything for either of you?'

'No, thank you.' Ben gave a quick smile, standing near the door with the police constable, as Ruby and I sat down. 'We shouldn't be here too long. There are just a few things that need clearing up. Dr Briggs examined Oliver's ankle and confirmed it's badly sprained but not broken. However, Oliver has made some rather serious accusations about your... um... husband. That is to say, Mr Stanley Miller.'

I swallowed as Ben struggled over the word 'husband'. It wasn't surprising; Ben had always known me as a single woman. Well, as single as a woman can be when she is married to a man who has deserted her. 'What sort of accusations?'

'Mr Beckwith claims Stan deliberately pushed him over the wall outside his office. He says it was an assault, and certainly not an accident.'

'That's ridiculous,' I said immediately, though it felt jolly strange to be the one defending Stan. 'Ben, I assure you that I saw the whole thing. Stan grabbed Oliver's arm to prevent him from walking away, and Oliver pulled back so forcefully that he lost his balance.'

'I suspected Mr Beckwith had not told PC Bottomley the whole story,' Ben said. 'Of course, I cannot divulge any details, but we do have reason to question the solicitor's honesty.'

'Have you spoken with Stan yet?'

'Not yet,' Ben confirmed. 'We thought it best to speak to you first and find out if there was any truth in Mr Beckwith's allegations before confronting him.'

'I'm afraid Stan had very good reason to confront Mr Beckwith,' I said. 'It seems that Stan arranged with the solicitor to send me a sum of money each month by way of support. As you know, I have never received a penny from Stan in his absence.'

'I see.' Ben looked pointedly at PC Bottomley, who raised his eyebrows in return. 'Perhaps you could take some notes?'

Cyril Bottomley patted his pockets. 'Oh dear. I wonder, could I trouble you for a pencil, Mrs Miller?'

Ruby jumped to her feet and looked at the rather dilatory village policeman. 'Will you need a notebook too, or do you have your own?'

'Thank you, Miss Andrews, but I have my police notebook.' He glanced quickly at Ben. 'I always have my notebook. Not sure where I've left my pencil.'

Ben, already quite accustomed to the bumbling policeman, nodded. 'Just a pencil, Ruby, thank you.'

Ruby made no attempt to hide her amusement as she crossed over to the bureau to get a pencil. 'Here we are. Will this take much longer? I'm famished.'

'Not much longer, then we shall leave you to your evening meal.' Ben turned back to me. 'Do you know where Stan is now?'

'He's staying at the Cricketer's Arms with two friends he has been staying with in Brighton.'

'Are we going to arrest him for wasting police time?' Cyril asked.

Ben looked at him in confusion. 'Who? Mr Miller, or Mr Beckwith?'

'Mr Miller, of course,' Cyril said with a definite air of frustration. 'If he left instructions with Mr Beckwith to send Mrs Miller maintenance, then he was never really a missing person, was he? The Metropolitan Police, as well as myself, spent countless hours trying to trace him. He should be arrested, in my opinion.'

Ben nodded. 'You have a very valid point.'

I hadn't even contemplated Stan being in trouble with the police for his own disappearance, but PC Bottomley was correct – a lot of time had been wasted looking for a man who had simply chosen to walk out of a life he didn't want any more and start anew somewhere else.

PC Bottomley practically preened at the praise. 'Thank you, sir.'

'Make a note of that. We shall discuss that with Mr Miller when we visit him.' Ben looked back at me. 'Is there anything else you think I should know?'

'The friends I mentioned, Ted and Bernard Harland, were also present during the altercation between Stan and Mr Beckwith. I'm sure they will agree with my recollection of the events.'

Ben nodded. 'That's very helpful. Right, I think that's everything for now. Thank you for your time.'

After the two men had left, Ruby and I went back into the kitchen. 'I wonder what Ben meant by they had "reason to question the solicitor's honesty".'

I shrugged. 'It seems he hasn't dealt with Stan in good faith, so perhaps there are other clients who have made similar complaints about his services.'

'It's a good job PC Bottomley has Ben to keep him in line,' Ruby said proudly. 'I'm sure he will get to the bottom of what is going on.'

'I'm sure you're right,' I said with a glance at the clock. 'Let's eat. If you're to meet Luke at Village Edge at seven, you will need to hurry.'

* * *

After we had eaten, and I had tidied the kitchen, I tried to settle down with a book, but the words blurred together on the page. My mind kept returning to the events of the day – Stan's seemingly changed personality, Oliver's apparent dishonesty, and Luke's desperate declaration. It felt as though the careful life I had built for myself since Stan's departure was crumbling around me.

Lizzy padded over and rested her head on my knee, sensing

my distress. I stroked her soft ears, grateful for her uncomplicated affection.

'What do you think, girl?' I asked softly. 'How does one choose between duty and love? Between what's safe and what's right?'

Lizzy's only response was to settle more comfortably against my legs, apparently content to leave such complex decisions to humans.

I forced myself to think about a safer subject and settled on the cricket match scheduled for the next day. It would be so strange to see Stan playing for the village team and representing the community he had once been so eager to escape. Meanwhile Oliver Beckwith would be nursing his injured pride, as well as his sprained ankle.

My mind wandered to Luke, as it so often did. What was he thinking? Did he regret his words to me earlier, or did he mean what he said?

The sound of the front door opening interrupted my brooding. Ruby's voice called out, cheerful and bright. 'Martha? I'm back! And you'll never guess who I met on my way home from Village Edge.'

I set aside my book and went to meet her in the hallway. Ruby's cheeks were flushed with cold and excitement. 'Who did you meet?'

'Martha!' A tall figure moved forward with speed and enveloped me in a warm hug.

'Annie, it's so good to see you again,' I said, my voice muffled against my friend's chest.

'Your sister has told me all about the goings on today. I'll never understand people who say villages are boring. There's always something happening.'

'I couldn't agree more.' I turned to Ruby. 'Did Luke bless the house?'

'He did.' She beamed happily. 'And I immediately felt a sense of complete calm. I know Ben thinks I'm a little batty, but I feel so much better about living there now.'

'That's the most important thing.' We sat around the kitchen table. 'Now, do tell me what has been going on in Winteringham.'

'Not much since my last letter,' Annie admitted. 'Though it's a strange coincidence that my friend, Lavinia Thompson, has come with me for the match and now Stan has returned.'

Ruby turned to me. 'Lavinia Thompson? Isn't that the lady Stan was walking out with before he married you?'

Was it a coincidence? Was Lavinia Thompson the real reason Stan was back in Westleham? Was it because Stan really wanted to marry Lavinia that he settled for me? Stan had always said that it was his choice to break things off with Lavinia but perhaps she was the reason our marriage had been unhappy.

I tried to shake my negative feelings away and attempted to look unconcerned as I answered Ruby's question. 'It is.'

'He completely broke her heart when he upped and married you and cast her aside,' Annie said with no hint of shame at sharing the gossip.

Well, that answered most of my concerns, though it didn't explain why Stan had never seemed happy with me. 'Oh, my goodness, really? Stan did tell me they were not well suited.'

'She's very quiet,' Annie said. 'The complete opposite to me, actually. It's probably why we get along so well. She's a seamstress, an extremely good one. She even dyes her own threads and material. But, as I said, devastated even to this day about Stan.'

'Surely she's had another beau since Stan?' Ruby asked. 'It's been years.'

'No,' Annie confirmed. 'No one.'

'Does she know Stan is back?' I asked cautiously.

'Oh yes.' Annie nodded. 'We're staying at the Cricketer's Arms too. Everyone is talking about Stan pushing over that solicitor.'

I should have had some sort of reaction to finding out my husband and his former beau were staying at the same establishment, but I didn't. My complete lack of emotion over learning that fact simply reiterated how dead my marriage was. 'Have you seen him?'

'Not yet, though not through want of trying. Lavinia has even been sitting in the lounge of the pub hoping he would come in. She knows we're friends, of course, and I've told her that he treated you quite dreadfully by running off and leaving you penniless. Silly woman still seems to think the man is worthy of her affections.'

'But he's married,' I said, not knowing how else to answer. 'To me.'

'I know.' Annie shook her head. 'It's a perfectly frightful situation all around. Lavinia still holds a torch for Stan and you hold a torch for Luke. If only we could go back in time and make sure Stan didn't throw Lavinia over, everyone would be happy.'

I doubted Lavinia would have made Stan happy. It seemed to me that living in Brighton with his friends, and having no family responsibilities, suited him much more than marriage.

Annie chattered on for a little longer, but she seemed to realise quickly that I was not my usual self. I found it hard to concentrate on what she was saying. All I could think about was what she had said about going back in time. Not for the first time, I lamented how jolly unfair life could be.

Later that evening, as I prepared for bed, I couldn't stop the day's events from going around in my head. I gave a shudder as I thought about all the different emotions that were swirling around: love, jealousy, dishonesty, greed, and possibly even violence.

I had the feeling that tomorrow would bring more questions than answers, and more complications than solutions. I could only hope for calm, but the storm of emotions swirling around the village hinted that disaster was inevitable.

4

The next morning dawned bright and clear, and for that I was glad. Annie and I had spent so long organising the day, rain would have completely ruined it.

I left Ruby to finish getting ready and walked with Lizzy through the village. Clifford Baker, who owned the post office that doubled as a grocery store, waved at me, and my heart sank. He was not known as a particularly friendly person, so the only reason I could think of for his cheery greeting that morning was because he wanted to find out what he could from me. Contrary to popular opinion, it wasn't just the old ladies in a village that liked to be up to date with gossip.

'Fine day for cricket, Mrs Miller. I hear your husband will be playing for our side today.'

Our side. I didn't know how he dared. When Luke and I had asked him about joining the team earlier this year, he professed to know nothing about cricket and wasn't at all interested in either joining the team or helping out in any way.

'Yes, so I understand,' I replied, still struggling to come to terms with the words 'your husband' being used in the present tense – I had got so used to Stan not being around.

'Haven't seen him play before. Hope he's up to the standard. Winteringham's got some decent bowlers, from what I hear.'

No doubt he had picked that information up in the Cricketer's Arms the previous evening. I made some noncommittal response and hurried on my way. I had no desire to add any more fuel to the village gossip.

Clifford's words stayed with me, and I realised I had no idea whether Stan was actually any good at cricket. I knew he had played at university, but that told me nothing about his current abilities. What if he made a fool of himself? Or worse, what if he proved to be brilliant and became the hero of the match? I wasn't sure which possibility disturbed me more, especially when I was rather expecting Luke to be the best player in Westleham's team.

Farmer Bennington's four sons were playing. They were all big, strapping young men, so good things were expected from them with bat in hand.

'Martha!' I turned to see Ada Garrett hurrying towards me. That is, Ada Bennington, as she now was. I was rather proud of my matchmaking between the war widow and the farmer. Though, of course, Maud now claimed the suggestion was entirely her own.

'Good morning, Mrs Bennington.'

Ada flushed. 'Every time someone calls me that, I want to look around and see who it is they are talking to.'

'I suppose it must take some getting used to.'

'It really does.' Ada smiled. 'It was all such a whirlwind. Though, at our age, there was little point in wasting time with a long courtship.'

Ada was only a few years older than me, John Bennington in

his forties, yet Ada had managed to make them sound as old as Maud.

'How are the children?'

Ada's face shone with happiness. 'They are all wonderful. My boys are really looking forward to playing cricket today. I've taught them everything Harry ever told me about the game.'

Harry had been Ada's first husband. Before the war, he had been the captain of the cricket team. Sadly, he had not returned home from the conflict, a fact that had made Ada very bitter. Our initial exchanges had not been positive, but we had quickly learned we had a lot in common and, together with Maud, had become fast friends.

I couldn't help but be a little jealous of Ada referring to farmer Bennington's sons as 'her boys'. Ada and I had always wanted children, and neither of us had been blessed. Now she had five who all seemed to adore her. I didn't think it was only because she was an absolute whizz in the kitchen. There was nothing Ada couldn't turn her hand to.

'That's wonderful, Ada. I hear Winteringham's bowlers are very good.'

'Humph,' Ada retorted. 'We'll see about that. My boys will soon show them!'

I couldn't fault either her maternal pride or her faith in her new stepsons. The same could be said every time Ada spoke about the one girl in the family. 'How is Shirley?'

'Oh, you should taste her pastry, Martha. Honestly, the girl is a natural. I only have to show her something once, and she's mastered it. She'll be a better cook than me by Christmas.'

I doubted that, but again, Ada's happiness in her new role was plain to see. 'Luke raved about the apple pie you sent over last weekend.'

'All Shirley's work.' Ada's face suddenly turned serious, and she leaned closer to me. 'I hate to ask, with all you have going on, but I really need some advice.'

'It would be a pleasure to help, if I can,' I said. 'And, quite honestly, a relief to think about something other than Stan, Oliver Beckwith, and what might go wrong next.'

'I have become aware that Frank has been seeing a lot of Iris.'

I could immediately see Ada's dilemma. Iris was Luke's sister, Frank the eldest of the Bennington boys. Until her parents had sent her away to work in London, Frank had been having a secret relationship with the publican's daughter, Florence Noble.

'And you think Luke doesn't know?'

'I'm certain he doesn't.'

'Why doesn't Frank just go to the vicarage and ask Luke if he can take Iris out?' I asked. 'Honesty really is the best policy, and I'm sure Luke would appreciate Frank being up front about his courtship rather than sneaking around.'

'I've told him the same thing myself.' Ada sighed. 'But after Winnie Noble made it clear she didn't think he was good enough for her daughter, the poor lad has no confidence in himself.'

Given she was obviously so fond of the lad, I didn't like to point out that he was clearly not lacking in confidence when it came to girls if he was seeing Iris regularly.

'As her father is in prison for a myriad of fraud offences, I hardly think Frank has anything to worry about with Luke. He's a hardworking boy from a good family. Frank really should speak to Luke before the two of them are found out. You know how it is in Westleham. Before too much longer, someone will see them together and tell Luke.'

'You're right, I know you are.' Ada patted my arm. 'I'll have another talk to Frank today. He might listen when he knows what you've said. Now—'

'Martha!' Ruby panted as she rushed up to us. 'There you are.'

'What's wrong?' Lizzy strained on the lead to welcome Ruby as I tried desperately not to panic; various reasons for my sister coming to find me, not ten minutes after I'd left the house, were racing through my mind.

'Stan wants his cricket equipment.'

'Did he come to the house?'

'He did,' Ruby said. 'And I refused to let him in.'

'Good for you,' Ada said approvingly.

'Ruby, it's his house.'

'Maybe so. But I didn't want him in it when you weren't there.'

I could imagine Ruby at the door standing up to Stan, and admiration for my sister flooded through me. I wouldn't have dared be so bold. 'What did he say?'

'He was actually very nice about it,' Ruby admitted. 'He just asked if you would mind bringing everything along to the pavilion at your earliest convenience.'

'At my earliest convenience?' I raised an eyebrow. 'Did he really say that?'

'His exact words,' Ruby confirmed. 'Give me Lizzy, and I'll walk her. You go back to the house, take Stan his things, then stay at the village green. I'll join you there.'

'Would you like me to come with you?' Ada asked, looking at me in concern.

'No.' I forced a smile. 'It's fine. I can manage. There's nothing wrong with me, I assure you. It's just a shock Stan being back. And being so reasonable.'

'I'm sure it is,' Ada said doubtfully. 'Well, if you're certain you don't need my company, I'd better get along and round up the children.'

'Children,' Ruby mouthed behind Ada's back and grinned. Neither of us were going to be the one to tell Ada that, at fifteen, Shirley was the only one of her new stepchildren who could legitimately be called a child, and even then I doubted she would like hearing herself referred to in that way.

* * *

Stan was standing near the pavilion with Ted and Bernard as I hurried forward with his cricket equipment.

'Oh, Mrs Miller!' Ted exclaimed. 'Do let me help you with that. How on earth did you manage to get over the road with your hands so full?'

A little bit of the old resentment I had felt at being left to cope with everything by myself when Stan left bubbled to the surface. I allowed Ted to take the pads and bat, and I handed Stan the gloves and his cricket whites.

'I'm quite resourceful,' I said.

'Indeed you are,' Ted praised with a smile.

'Oh, gosh, there's that dreadfully dull woman,' Bernard remarked with a barely suppressed shudder.

I turned to see Annie and Lavinia approaching. Annie could be described in many different ways, but dull was definitely not a label that could be applied to her. That meant he must have been referring to Lavinia.

'Who's that?' Stan asked as he inspected his kit.

'Lavinia whatsherface,' Bernard said. 'Didn't you say you were engaged to her, or something?'

'Oh, my goodness, no.' Stan laughed. Clearly, he had not heard the start of the conversation, as he made no attempt to lower his voice. 'She hinted so wildly that she wanted us to get engaged that it quite put me off her. I had thought her a timid little thing, but I'm afraid the keener on me she got, the more off-putting I found her.'

'Stan!' I hissed, completely stunned at his words. Although he was repeating what he had always told me about Lavinia, it wasn't like him to be so blunt.

'What are you doing, Ted?' Stan turned to his friend, who was quite forcefully stepping on one of Stan's feet.

'You must be Stan Miller,' Annie remarked, with the same warmth she might have shown the Kaiser. Her tone left no doubt that the two women had overheard everything Stan had said.

'Good morning, ladies,' Stan said in a voice so falsely bright that Ted winced. 'Do please excuse me, I must get changed.'

Stan hurried into the pavilion, true to form – creating a situation and then running from the mess he'd made.

* * *

'You look dreadful,' Maud said without a hint of contrition at her brutal honesty.

'I didn't get much sleep last night,' I admitted. 'I couldn't stop thinking about the cricket match and all the complications that go with it.'

'You don't fool me, Martha Miller.' Maud eyed me shrewdly. 'You're not worried about the cricket game at all. It's the two men in your life that are keeping you awake.'

'Don't say it like that,' I protested. 'That makes it sound like I'm trying to decide between them both.'

'Aren't you?' Maud raised an eyebrow.

'Of course not.' I shook my head for emphasis. 'You know which of them I would choose if circumstances were such that a choice could be made.'

'You already know what I think.'

'I do,' I said, because we'd had this conversation many times before. 'But you know it's not that simple. Luke's first obligation is to the Church.'

'We'll see,' she said cryptically.

I couldn't help but wonder if she'd been advising Luke and was the reason for his sudden declaration the previous day. 'Stan and Luke are not the only things on my mind. There's Oliver Beckwith, and his possibly illicit dealings to worry about. As if all that's not enough, Stan made some comments that Lavinia Thompson overheard, and she's run off crying.'

'What a ninny,' Maud said dismissively. 'Now, let's find somewhere to sit. There's Luke with the umpire and the Winteringham captain. It looks as though they're about to toss up.'

Ada had laid out a thick blanket and waved us over. Ruby was already sitting down, ready for the game to begin, Lizzy sleeping at her side.

'Everything all right?' Ruby asked, and I nodded.

'Look at Luke.' Maud clicked her tongue. 'He looks as though he's had about as much sleep as you, Martha.'

'Nonsense,' Ada said briskly with a look of sympathy my way. 'You can't see a thing from here, Maud Burnett!'

'I certainly can,' Maud retorted. 'My eyesight is excellent.'

'How many fingers has the umpire raised?' Ruby said with a grin in my direction.

Maud leaned forward, as though that would help her see more clearly, then realised Ruby was joking. 'Wait until he comes off then you'll see I'm right.'

'Oh, he won't be coming off until Westleham have finished batting,' Iris said. 'Is there room down there for another one?'

Iris was a thoroughly modern young woman who had come to live with Luke earlier that year. She had transformed the vicarage in a few short months and now, instead of parishioners wiping their feet on the way out, she ensured her brother lived in a neat and clean house fit for a vicar. The housekeeper, Gertrude Felton, rather than be embarrassed at her own slovenly work, seemed overjoyed she got paid for something Iris did for free.

Ruby slid a little closer to me to make room for Iris. When the other young woman sat down, Ruby gently nudged her with her elbow. 'Does your brother know about you and Frank Bennington?'

'How do y—' She glared at Ada.

'Don't blame Mrs Bennington,' Ruby said. 'If you don't want your relationship to be common knowledge in the village, I suggest you carry on somewhere a little more private than behind the oak tree opposite Village Edge.'

'You saw us,' Iris said flatly.

'I saw you,' Ruby confirmed. 'I walked Lizzy this morning and, let me tell you, you weren't hard to miss.'

Iris held her hands up to her red cheeks. 'Please don't tell my brother.'

'He won't hear it from me,' Ruby assured her friend. 'But if you don't tell him soon, someone else will do it for you.'

'I've told Frank the same thing,' Ada said. 'Nothing good ever comes from keeping a secret like that.'

'What did you mean when you said Luke won't come off the field until the end?' I steered the conversation onto a neutral subject.

'My brother is awfully good at cricket,' Iris said proudly. 'He represented the county when he was at school. I believe he still holds the record for most runs in a season.'

'That doesn't surprise me one little bit,' Maud said with motherly pride. She wasn't his mother, of course, but she was very fond of him.

I looked around at the cricket green. Families had spread out blankets, just as we had. Children were running about, calling to each other with excitement. Joe Noble was setting up a table at the entrance to the green. In another half an hour or so, he would start serving drinks. Licensing laws would only allow him to serve until mid-afternoon, but, no doubt, his wife was hoping to make a good profit as everyone enjoyed the first cricket game since before the war.

The game began, with Luke scoring steadily, just as Iris had predicted. However, he quickly went through batting partners as one by one, the batsmen were summarily dispatched. The Bennington boys, to Ada's consternation, were out for a combined total of twelve. They all swung wildly and with great vigour – which would have been splendid had they managed to connect with the ball. As it was, one knocked off his own bails, one was caught by the wicketkeeper, and two were taken in the slips.

The final batsman was Stan. I couldn't help but feel nervous as he strode out onto the green from the pavilion with his bat tucked under one arm. He was still pulling on his gloves, such was the haste with which he had rushed from watching the game to preparing himself to bat.

He flexed his hands and took hold of his bat, swinging it casually by his side. He and Luke exchanged a few words before he made his way to the crease to face the Winteringham bowler. Unfortunately, it had soon transpired that the information Clifford Baker had given me earlier was correct – the bowlers were very good.

The Winteringham bowler began his run-up, and I held my breath as the ball flew towards my husband's waiting bat.

'Good luck, Stan,' Ted called.

'It's gone for six,' Maud said in obvious surprise. 'Martha, did you know Stan could play cricket?'

'I did not,' I said. 'He had all of the paraphernalia in his wardrobe, but he never mentioned to me that he even liked cricket.'

'Maybe it was a lucky first shot,' Ada suggested.

Stan walked a couple of steps, poked at his gloves as though they were too tight for him, and then readied himself for the next ball to head his way. It turned out that Stan's first shot was not lucky as, with a rather impressive thwack, he hit the ball again.

There was something rather satisfactory about the sound the bat made as it hit the ball. Villagers who had been disheartened by the unimpressive show of batting from the Westleham team up until that moment were suddenly very interested once more in the game.

Stan's second shot hit the boundary for a score of four.

As Stan was preparing to face his third ball, he seemed to stagger and put his bat on the floor, as though to regain his balance.

The crowd gave a collective gasp as Stan fell sideways, clutching at his chest.

For a moment, no one moved, and an unsettling quiet fell over the cricket green.

A woman shrieked loudly, which seemed to galvanise Luke into action. He ran towards Stan, who was writhing on the floor, pulling at his gloves.

Without a moment's thought, I ran to Stan's side. His face was flushed, his eyes wild, his right hand pressed to his chest while his left flailed, as though trying to shake off his cricket glove.

I reached forward and took it off, noticing as I did so that the skin on the palm of his left hand was red, as though he had burned it on an oven.

I looked over at Luke, but he refused to look my way as he spoke words of comfort to Stan.

A rushing filled my ears, drowning out everything else. The sounds around me became distant, muffled, as though they were coming from far away. Somewhere in the haze, I could hear someone calling out for the doctor.

To my absolute horror, I knew that it didn't matter how quickly Dr Briggs arrived – it would be too late.

My husband was dying right before my eyes.

5

My hearing cleared and although I no longer felt as though I was hearing things from an underwater cavern, the complete silence over the cricket green was just as strange. I looked up to what seemed like the entire village staring at me – some open-mouthed, some shaking their heads sadly, while others clearly didn't yet appreciate the full magnitude of what had happened.

'Martha.' Ruby knelt next to me and placed a hand on my arm. 'Come along, darling, we need to get you home.'

'I can't go home.' I shook my head defiantly. 'I need to stay here, with Stan, I can't leave him all alone.'

'Mrs Miller,' Dr Briggs said gently. 'I'm afraid Mr Miller has passed away. There's nothing either of us can do here.'

'You must do something.'

The doctor got to his feet and snapped his medical bag closed. The sharp sound seemed to echo across the entire village. 'I'm so sorry, but it's too late.'

'Too late?' I repeated. 'But it can't be. Stan was hitting fours and sixes. He was fine.'

'He wasn't fine, Martha,' Luke said.

'Wasn't he?' I asked in confusion.

'Before he started batting, he told me he felt a bit odd. He said his fingers were numb and he was a little dizzy.' Luke shook his head. 'The poor fellow passed it off as nerves because he hadn't played for so long.'

I had never known Stan to have a day's illness in his entire life. He had survived the war, and to my knowledge suffered no lingering ill effects. Unlike many poor soldiers who returned from war, Stan hadn't had any issues with his nerves either.

'Maybe I should—'

'Ruby's right.' Luke walked to my left and together, he and Ruby helped me to my feet. 'You need to go home. This has been a terrible shock for you.'

They supported me to the edge of the green. Ted Harland, his face leached of any colour, put out a hand to stop me. 'Mrs Miller, what is it? What has happened?'

'Mr Harland, is it?' Luke asked. 'I'm very sorry to have to tell you that your friend has passed away.'

Ben sprinted up to us, his hair mussed, his breath laboured. 'Martha, Luke, is what I've heard correct? Stan is dead?'

'I'm afraid so,' Luke said.

'Please stay here while I speak to the doctor. I'll be back in a moment.' Ben hurried onto the pitch and was soon in a conversation with Dr Briggs.

'Stan is dead?' Ted asked in obvious disbelief.

'He was doing so well,' I said. 'I had no idea Stan could play cricket like that.'

'That's because you don't know him.' Ted's eyes were bright with unshed tears. 'You never knew him like I know him.'

I stared at Ted, unable to think of a single thing to say in response. Mostly because I knew the man I married had never allowed me to know the real him. I had always known there were parts of Stan that he kept secret from me. He hadn't once spoken to me about his hopes and dreams for our future, about his job, about anything that was actually important.

And now I would never know those things because he was dead. Only yesterday he had returned to Westleham, and promised to transfer the house to me, and now, very suddenly, he was dead. None of it seemed real. Even as I tried to sort through my own confused feelings, I couldn't help but notice how very badly Ted was taking Stan's death.

Ben came back over. 'Dr Briggs will stay with Stan until the ambulance comes to take him to the hospital.'

'Ambulance?' Ted asked, hope evident in his voice. 'Then the doctor thinks something can be done for Stan?'

'I'm afraid not, Mr Harland. The ambulance will transport Stan to the mortuary.'

'Mortuary?' I repeated, unable to think clearly enough to form a coherent sentence. All I seemed to be doing since Stan's collapse was repeating little parts of what other people had said.

'Yes, Martha,' Ben said. 'Dr Briggs thinks there are suspicious circumstances.'

'It will be that solicitor. I'm certain he has done it to shut Stan up.' Ted waved a hand wildly. 'He'll be here somewhere, I have no doubt. Have you spoken to him yet? He was stealing from Stan and using the money Stan gave him for Mrs Miller for his own purposes. I insist you arrest him immediately for fraud, embezzlement, theft, and murder!'

Ben held up a hand. 'Calm down, Mr Harland. I can assure you that an investigation into Mr Beckwith's business dealings is already underway. I'm sure you can appreciate that I can't say any more than that at the present time.'

'What a terrible tragedy,' someone whispered. 'Poor Mrs

Miller. Despite him being away for so long, she looks quite devastated.'

Poor Mrs Miller: that's what they would all say now. The woman whose husband had abandoned her, only for him to return and then die before her eyes. I would be an object of pity once more, just when I had finally found my footing in the village.

'Suspicious circumstances?' I asked as Ben's words finally sank into my consciousness. 'Do you mean he was murdered? Is that what you're saying?'

'Of course that's what he's saying!' Ted snapped. 'You probably did it yourself so you can inherit all of his money.'

I gasped at his harsh words and shook my head in denial. 'No. Stan was going to transfer the house to me. Why would I kill him when he was giving me the house?'

It would have been false to profess love for Stan, yet I bore him no ill will. Even so, the thought that anyone might believe me capable of such a thing left me shaken. 'Why settle for a house, when you can have everything?'

'That's enough!' Maud stepped in between me and Stan's friend. 'I understand you have lost a friend, so we will excuse your behaviour, but can't you see poor Mrs Miller has lost her husband and is quite bereft.'

It didn't surprise me to hear Maud sticking up for me, but it did startle me to realise that she was right. I did feel absolutely inconsolable. Until that moment, I hadn't realised that I was crying. My hands shook and my legs felt wobbly as though I would fall to my knees without the support of Ruby and Luke.

'I apologise,' Ben said with a sympathetic look in my direction, 'but I'm going to have to ask you to go home. We need to clear the cricket green for the ambulance and I also need to seal the area off to preserve any evidence there may be.'

'A tot of whisky is what you need, my dear,' Maud said. 'For the shock. Let's get you home.'

'I'm sorry, Luke,' Ben said quietly, 'but I must insist that you go to the vicarage and not to Martha's house. You know what Westleham is like, there will be talk. Let's not give the villagers a reason to gossip about you.'

'Am I a suspect?' Luke asked incredulously.

'Everyone is a suspect,' Ben responded promptly. 'It's the way it has to be. I wouldn't be doing my job if I discounted a person simply because I had an existing relationship with them. In fact, I wouldn't be surprised if I am removed from the case given my close relationship.'

'Quite right too,' Ted said. 'I won't let you all conspire with each other. Stan deserves his death to be investigated impartially. Oh, what shall I do—'

'Let's go back to the Cricketer's Arms.' Bernard put an arm around his brother. 'Staying here and arguing with these people isn't helping anyone, least of all Stan.'

The two men left together and I looked back at Stan's prone body. How could a day that held such promise have ended so terribly?

* * *

Ruby insisted on making tea while I sat at the kitchen table, still wearing my best dress that was now stained with grass and dirt from kneeling beside Stan's body. Lizzy sensed my distress and pressed her warm flank against my legs, offering what comfort she could.

'I can't believe he's gone,' I said for the third time since we'd returned home. 'And so terribly.'

'I know.' Ruby set a steaming cup before me. 'It's a terrible shock.'

Maud came bustling through the back door holding a bottle of whisky, and her knitting bag. She pushed the cup of tea Ruby made me onto the side. 'She doesn't want that, Ruby, she needs a good stiff drink for the shock.'

I surprised myself. 'Actually, I think I'll have both.'

'Ruby?' Maud held up the bottle, tilting it with a questioning lift of her brow, as she put a couple of glasses on the table and poured a measure for the two of us.

'Not for me, thank you. It's a bit early for me.'

Maud nodded sagely. 'That's probably a wise decision.'

Ruby shifted uncomfortably in her chair as Maud got out her knitting. Although I tried hard to knit, I wasn't very good. Ruby, to my knowledge, had never been interested to learn. Within moments, the only sound in the kitchen was Maud's needles clacking together in a wonderfully rhythmic cadence I could never achieve myself.

I picked up the small tot and drank it, knowing I would hate the taste but hoping the sharp bite of the alcohol might snap me out of the fugue state I was in. A brisk rap at the door interrupted our conversation. Ruby hurried to answer it, returning with Ben.

'Martha, I need to speak with you privately,' he said.

'Of course,' I said with no attempt to hide my reluctance. 'We can go through to the lounge.'

I led the way and sat in the chair next to the window. Ben closed the door behind him, looking almost as uncomfortable as I felt. This couldn't be easy for him.

He shuffled his feet before clearing his throat. 'What can you tell me about what you saw?'

'You didn't see?' I had a vague recollection of Ben hurrying up to the cricket green after the incident had taken place.

'No, I was talking to Oliver Beckwith at his home.'

'Had you been there with him long?'

Ben held up a hand. 'Martha, no. Don't do that. You can't question me, that's my job. Please don't involve yourself in this investigation. I've tolerated it in the past because I know you mean well. However, I'm certain I'll be taken off this case, and my replacement may not take kindly to you snooping around the village.'

I tried not to take offence at Ben's words while clamping my lips together, so I didn't point out that my 'snooping' had directly led to three cases being solved. 'Am I a suspect?'

'As I told Luke, everyone is a suspect.'

'But you know me.'

'I do,' Ben said, his tone edged with sadness. 'Which is why I'm certain I won't be in charge of this investigation. I do know that you couldn't have done this, Martha, I really do. But someone from the outside, coming in, will look at the fact that Stan was back in the village after being away for nearly two years, the cricket equipment was stored in your home, and then there's Luke.'

'But nothing—'

Ben shook his head. 'No one has seen anything improper happen between you and Luke. However, as Maud would say, anyone with eyes in their head can see that you care about each other. All it takes is for someone to tell whoever is in charge, and you've got the motive and the opportunity.'

'Have I got the means, too?'

'I don't know,' Ben admitted. 'That depends on what the doctors at the hospital say. There will have to be some specific tests on Stan's body, though Dr Briggs has a good idea of the cause of death.'

'Which is?' I looked at his impassive face and gave a small nod. 'You can't share that information with me.'

'This isn't easy for me, Martha. I respect you, but I must do my duty.'

'I understand.'

While I understood Ben's predicament, because he had only spoken the truth, I needed to look at what had happened from a selfish point of view. I could see that someone new coming in to investigate Stan's death would naturally position me as a suspect because of what I would have to gain. Then there was Ted's outspoken attack on me on the cricket green. It was possible he was letting his emotions run away with him but that didn't mean people wouldn't listen to his accusations and think he had a point.

I was all too well aware how gossip could spread around a village such as Westleham. It would only take a few people to repeat Ted's accusation for some people to believe I was as guilty as he had suggested.

'How well do you know the two brothers Stan was staying with? I assume you only met them yesterday?'

'That's right. Stan seemed happy when he came back. Certainly happier than he ever was living in Westleham with me,' I admitted sadly. 'Ted accused me of killing Stan.'

'Yes, I heard that accusation.'

'I'm certain he will repeat it.' The measure of whisky gave me bravery that, until that moment, had laid dormant since Stan's death. Or perhaps the shock was wearing off and I was feeling more like myself. 'However, what he won't have told you is that his brother is a pharmacist. I heard Bernard tell Mr Beckwith that when he had his accident.'

'What is the relevance to that information, Martha?' Ben

raised an eyebrow at me, but I knew him well enough by now to know he was bluffing.

'Stan died suddenly. Dr Briggs thinks there's foul play. So that rules out a heart attack or some other natural cause. He wasn't stabbed, or shot, so that really leaves us with some sort of poison, doesn't it? And that, I believe, brings us rather neatly to Bernard Harland who in his line of work would have a good knowledge of poisons.'

'I am making no comment on your suggestion.' Ben worked hard at keeping a neutral expression. 'Do you think Stan was close to Ted and Bernard?'

'They seemed fond of each other, from what I could tell. Even knowing Bernard's profession, it's hard to imagine either of them killing Stan.'

'Sometimes the people closest to us have the most to gain from our deaths, Martha. Or the most to lose from our revelations.'

The truth of that statement settled over me like a shroud. If Stan had discovered something about his friends' activities in Brighton – something serious enough to threaten their livelihoods or freedom – they might indeed have reasons to silence him permanently.

But equally, so could I. My entire life had taken a complete turn in those few minutes it had taken Stan to die. I was no longer a deserted wife waiting for her husband's return. I was a widow, free to make my own choices about the future.

Under different circumstances, that might have been a relief, but knowing that someone had murdered Stan – someone who might still be walking free in our village – cast a shadow over any hope of happiness.

'One last question before I leave you.' Ben looked almost as awkward as he had the night he had come to the house to ask for permission to marry Ruby. 'I don't suppose you would know if Stan made a will?'

I didn't pretend to misunderstand the reason behind Ben's question. If I knew Stan had a will, and everything was left to me, I would look more guilty. If I knew he hadn't made a will, the same applied, because, as his wife, I was his legal next of kin.

'He never spoke to me of making a will. He could have made one here in Westleham, or even after he left, but I'm afraid I wouldn't know.'

'Yet Ted seemed to think you would inherit everything. That was certainly the impression he gave.'

I met Ben's gaze. 'Then that's really a question you need to ask him, isn't it?'

'You can be certain I will. I'll do as much as I can to find the perpetrator before I'm replaced. You can be certain of that, Martha.'

I nodded but couldn't find the words to give a proper answer. I wasn't angry at Ben; he was doing exactly what he should. However, my emotions were so close to the surface, it was hard to keep them in check. Despite my difficult relationship with Stan, it was hard to stop crying.

Ben left me in the parlour, and I heard him go through to the kitchen, no doubt to say goodbye to Ruby. I couldn't stop thinking about the red mark on Stan's palm, the way he had adjusted his gloves as he'd come onto the field, Luke saying Stan had said his fingers were numb, his collapse, and the way he had desperately tried to remove the glove from his left hand. I wasn't a medical expert by any stretch of the imagination but it certainly appeared to me that something had been added to Stan's glove.

It seemed so unfair that he was enjoying a pastime he hadn't participated in since his youth and it was that activity that had killed him. It also hadn't escaped my attention that Luke was the one who had encouraged Stan to replace Oliver in the team.

What should have been a time of joy for Stan had been turned against him, changing a happy moment into the instrument of his death. The realisation filled me with a cold fury that surprised me. Stan and I had not been happy together, but he had been trying to make amends. He deserved the chance to build a better life, even if that life didn't include me.

Someone had stolen that chance from him, and I was determined to see that they paid for it.

* * *

I waited for the front door to click shut behind Ben before I went back into the kitchen.

'Goodness, Martha, you look better.'

'I think the whisky helped.' I smiled at Maud. 'Now, who's ready for a bit of sleuthing?'

'Ah.'

'What does "ah" mean?' I looked at Ruby.

'Ben specifically said we were not to meddle.'

I lifted a shoulder and held out my hands. 'He's said that every time we've been around a murder and I haven't listened to him yet.'

'That's true.'

'But? I hear the but in your voice, Ruby.'

'But this time it's a little too close to home, isn't it?'

I didn't hesitate. 'Yes. Which is exactly why we must find out who did it. Ben pointed out that I have both the motive and the opportunity – I'm not waiting for the results of the tests at the mortuary for someone to decide I also have the means. I'm going to uncover the real murderer before those tests come back.'

'Do you know what happened to him?' Ruby asked.

'I don't know,' I admitted. 'But I strongly suspect and when I posited that theory to Ben, he didn't tell me I was wrong.'

'What was it?' Maud put down her needles. 'What killed Stan?'

'Poison.' I pointed towards my back garden. 'Everyone in the village knows I am a keen gardener.'

'But you grow vegetables, Martha,' Ruby interjected. 'Not poison.'

'I do but the insinuation will be because I know about plants, I would know which ones could be used as a poison. I don't think it would be necessary for them to actually grow in my garden, but if there's some nearby, that will be enough for me to fly to the top of the suspect list. Especially if Stan hasn't made a new will since leaving Westleham and I'm to inherit everything.'

'Is he rich?' Maud asked with a very interested gleam in her eyes.

'I don't know,' I said. 'But he has enough money to pay off the mortgage on this house. Then Ted said "why would I settle for the house when I could have it all" so I assume Stan must have had more in the bank than the house money.'

'It'll be nice for you to have a little nest egg and no husband,' Maud commented. 'My understanding is that vicars are very poorly paid.'

Ruby and I looked at each other in shock. 'It's a bit soon.'

Maud wagged her finger at Ruby. 'I was simply making an observation. Do not tell me that the same thought hadn't already occurred to you.'

'Don't you want to know how Stan was poisoned?' I turned the conversation away from money, dead husbands, and attractive vicars. Not only was it too soon to think how this event would affect the rest of my life, it terrified me to even allow my thoughts to head in Luke's direction.

'I certainly do,' Ruby said.

Maud picked her knitting back up. 'It sounds as though you have a theory.'

'I do,' I told them. 'Stan looked uncomfortable in his gloves, he complained to Luke that his fingers felt numb, and after his collapse he was trying desperately to take his left glove off. When I removed it for him, there was a red mark on his hand as though something had been irritating it.'

'What was it?' Ruby asked as she leaned closer.

'Monkshood,' Maud said quickly.

'I would agree.' I nodded. 'It's a deadly poison and grows in many different areas all around the village.'

'That's rather scary,' Ruby commented.

'It's only deadly if you touch its roots or leaves without wearing gardening gloves,' I said. 'There isn't any in our garden, but there's plenty in the area. It's actually a rather pretty plant. Gorgeous bluey purple flowers.'

'And you think someone put the poison into Stan's cricket gloves?' Maud asked sagely.

'I do.' I nodded. 'Which could well be half the village. After all, the pavilion is never locked, and people were going in and out all day to get ready to bat. The problem for me, of course, is that I carried Stan's things over this morning.'

'Oh dear.' Ruby looked at me with a worried expression. 'No wonder you and Ben are so worried.'

'Indeed. I understand why Ben doesn't want me to investigate, and I'll do my very best not to impede the investigation – whether it's carried out by Ben or someone else. But I must do it. People here in Westleham will say things to me that they would never say to a police detective from Reading.'

'Who will you start with?'

'Oliver Beckwith,' I said immediately. 'Not only has he been withholding money from me, but I can enquire whether or not he has a will for Stan. That would be my right to ask as Stan's widow.' Hearing my spoken words caused a shiver to run down my spine. How strange it was to think of myself as a widow.

A quiet tap sounded on the front door and Ruby turned to me. 'Who can that be now?'

'I don't think I've ever had so many visitors in twenty-four hours.'

Ruby soon returned with Iris, who looked rather excited. 'I've been sent on a mission.'

'Well don't just stand there trembling, girl, what is the mission?' Maud asked. She held something out to me and I took it, then looked down. 'You've hurried over here to bring me a knitting pattern? For a balaclava?'

'It's a helmet liner,' Maud said, seeing Iris and Ruby's confused faces. 'They fitted underneath a soldier's helmet and helped to keep them warm.'

'Have you brought me this for a reason?'

'Well of course.' Iris smiled brightly at me. 'Luke was working in his office, I was tidying around, then Detective Inspector Robertson arrived. Luke asked for some privacy, and suggested I bring over the knitting pattern you asked for, and passed it to me.'

'I still don't understand.'

'Luke was at his desk. Writing.'

'Oh,' I said as the penny finally dropped. I opened the pattern to find a handwritten note inside. 'Luke has sent me a letter.'

'Concealed in a knitting pattern.' Maud took off her glasses and began rubbing them on the hem of her dress. 'How romantic.'

My breath caught as I unfolded the note to see Luke's now familiar handwriting.

My dear Martha,

I am praying for you – that you may find the strength to face this dark time with your usual courage and good sense. I grieve for Stan's passing, and for the burden it lays upon you.

Please remember that you are always in my thoughts and prayers.

Always.

Luke.

I folded the paper and put it in my pocket. 'Tell your brother I said thank you for the pattern, it was exactly what I needed.'

'I will.' She hesitated then said quickly, 'And, Martha, I'm so sorry for what has happened. I truly am.'

After Iris left, I turned to Ruby and Maud. 'I'm going to get changed. Then I think I will visit Oliver Beckwith.'

'Splendid idea.' Maud nodded in approval. 'Ruby, perhaps you can put on a little more lipstick, then take Iris some of that wool she asked for?'

'Wool? Lipstick? What on earth are you talking about?'

Maud sighed and reached into her knitting bag, bringing out a ball of lemon wool. 'Here, take this. Freshen up your lipstick, dear, and go over to the vicarage. See if you can't detain your lovely fiancé for half an hour, there's a dear.'

As I went up the stairs to my bedroom, I couldn't help but smile at Maud's antics. She really was an exceptionally good friend.

I took great care to put the note from Luke into the pocket of my clean dress, laying the one I had been wearing when Stan died on my bed. I knew with certainty that I wouldn't wear that dress ever again.

6

I wasn't sure if Oliver Beckwith would even see me but, with Maud at my side, I was more confident in my abilities to start investigating Stan's death.

As Stan's widow, it was my right to discuss his affairs with the village solicitor. My new status afforded me a certain authority I had lacked only that morning. It was a strange and bitter thought.

Maud and I made our way through the village towards Oliver Beckwith's house, and I was certain every pair of curtains twitched as we passed. Convention might demand that I remain at home in mourning, but I no longer felt I had that luxury.

I was no longer just Martha Miller, the abandoned wife; I was now Martha Miller, the tragic widow. Or, depending on who was doing the whispering, Martha Miller, the prime suspect.

Oliver Beckwith lived in a large thatched cottage around the corner from his office. It was a property that spoke of long-established respectability, even if its owner now seemed to lack it. I took hold of the brass knocker and knocked firmly on the dark green door.

A moment later, the door was opened by Oliver himself. He leaned heavily on a walking stick, his left foot neatly bandaged. He did not wear his usual immaculate suit but instead was dressed in neatly pressed trousers, with a mustard-coloured cardigan buttoned over his shirt. His expression soured the moment he saw me.

'Mrs Miller, Mrs Burnett,' he said, his tone unwelcoming. 'This isn't a convenient time.'

'I'm sure it isn't, Mr Beckwith,' I replied, my voice steadier than I felt. 'But I imagine very little about today has been convenient for anyone. May we please come in?'

'I don't see clients on a Saturday.' He kept a firm hold of the door, as though he believed I would barge past him into his home. 'And definitely not in my private residence.'

He made it sound as though he lived in Buckingham Palace instead of a four-bedroomed cottage in Westleham.

'We're not clients,' Maud returned and pushed his arm away, sweeping past him as if he had invited us. 'We have come to ask a perfectly legitimate question about a will. After which, it's possible we – at least Mrs Miller – will become a client.'

'Really, Mrs Burnett—' he began, but I had already followed Maud into the narrow hall. 'This is most irregular. I am not a well man. I must insist—'

'You're right,' Maud said breezily. 'We all really must sit down. It can't be very comfortable for you standing on that bad ankle.'

'It's not. Let me tell you, it's jolly painful.' Oliver grimaced as though suddenly in the grip of immense pain. 'One shouldn't speak badly of the dead but Mr Miller did attack me like he was possessed by the very devil himself.'

'What nonsense,' I retorted. 'He barely touched you.'

The solicitor made a tsking noise and led us along the corridor, past a room that I believed was his parlour, and opened a door on the left. He stood back to let us enter before him.

The room, clearly his study, smelled of floor polish and old paper. Oliver sat on the chair behind his desk. Maud didn't wait for him to invite her to sit. I chose to remain standing. I wasn't sure that it gave me any sort of an advantage but it made me feel better to look down on the man that I was certain was responsible for keeping me short of money for nearly two years.

'I have come to ask about my late husband's affairs,' I said firmly. 'Specifically, I need to know if you hold a will for him.'

Oliver's eyes narrowed. 'My dealings with your husband remain confidential despite his untimely demise. You may not be aware that there is an expectation of client confidentiality between a solicitor and his client.'

'Then he was your client?'

'I think we both know that he was.'

'So I shall ask again: did my husband make a will with your firm or, perhaps, elsewhere?'

'Mr Miller's private affairs are none of your business.'

'Hogwash,' Maud spluttered. 'She is his widow. Who else's business is it if not hers? You may not recall but when Mr Burnett passed away, Lord bless his soul, you were at my door brandishing his will practically begging that your firm be engaged to handle the probate.'

'That's not at all how I remember it,' Oliver blustered.

'It is fact,' Maud insisted. 'Now, please answer the question with as much honesty as you can manage. We are well aware that isn't one of your strong points. For some reason known only to yourself, you refused to pay a deserted wife money which was left with you specifically for her support. A matter, let me assure you, of which the police are well aware.'

'My dear lady—' Oliver began in his oily voice.

'I'm not your dear anything,' Maud cut in. 'Now stop with your blathering, and tell us what we want to know.'

'Mrs Miller,' the solicitor said, addressing me. 'There has clearly been a mistake with regard to the maintenance money your husband left in my keeping. Some sort of clerical issue, I believe, that you can be sure I will be discussing with my secretary on Monday. For that, I apologise.'

'And the will, Mr Beckwith?'

He opened a desk drawer and withdrew a cheque book. 'There is no will, Mrs Miller. At least, not here, neither one executed by me nor kept here in our strongroom.'

I was rather surprised at that revelation. It was strange that Stan had taken the time to consult with the solicitor about leaving money to support me when he left the village, yet had not made a will at the same time.

'Why have you never said you knew Stan intended to leave Westleham?'

Oliver Beckwith uncapped his fountain pen before looking in my direction. 'For the same reason I gave you earlier. Client confidentiality. It was not my responsibility to tell anyone that your husband was alive and well and had left the village of his own free will.'

'I didn't know whether he was dead or alive.' To my horror, my voice cracked and tears pricked behind my eyes. 'The police questioned everyone about his disappearance, yet still you said nothing.'

'Client confidentiality,' he repeated. 'It takes precedence over everything.'

I shook my head, afraid that if I tried to tell him how abhorrent I found his reasoning I would start crying once more. Surely I'd already cried enough tears for a man I hadn't loved for some time – if ever.

'What is that you're doing?' Maud asked suspiciously.

With a flourish that might have impressed other people – but was quite lost on Maud and me – Oliver signed, tore the cheque from his book along the perforation, and handed it to me.

I looked at the sum of money written in the box above the solicitor's rapidly drying signature and swallowed. 'What is this?'

'As I've just told you,' he said smoothly, 'there has been some sort of error at my firm, for which I take full responsibility. The cheque represents the sum of money you ought to have received in your husband's absence.'

I masked my shock at the amount by pressing him further. 'But not the whole of the sum my husband deposited with you before he left the village?'

He smiled, though it carried no comfort – instead it called to mind a reptile poised to devour its prey. 'That is correct. The remaining balance will, of course, be held by me until your husband's estate has been proved in probate. At that time, once the rightful heir is certain, the money will be released.'

'I see.' I folded the cheque and slipped it into my pocket, where it pressed against Luke's letter. 'I'm thankful your firm's error has been corrected, and for that I am obliged. But I do not believe your dishonesty will go unpunished.'

'As I have said, it was an honest mistake,' he replied, his smile thin. 'And since the only person who might have brought the matter before the Law Society is, regrettably, no longer with us, I think you will find the matter closed.'

'On the contrary,' I replied, letting as much derision creep into my voice as I could. 'I think the police are already very interested in pursuing charges against you. The fact that Mr Miller is "no longer with us" will only add to their suspicions.'

The solicitor's calm façade slipped, giving way to panic. 'My wife told me it was sudden, and appeared natural. Surely his death was from a heart attack?'

'I must say no more,' I answered. 'But I am certain you will be hearing from Detective Inspector Robertson before long.'

He paled, his bluster crumbling into fear. 'I had nothing to do with his death. Nothing! It must have been a terrible accident. I am a solicitor, not some deviant who goes about killing men on cricket fields.'

Perhaps not – but Oliver Beckwith was a thief and a liar. I had confirmed his motive, and had no doubt he had the nerve to plan Stan's murder. Whether or not he had the knowledge required remained to be seen.

* * *

'Thank you,' I said to Maud as the solicitor closed his front door behind us. 'You didn't let Mr Beckwith browbeat you, and it gave me the courage to say what I needed to.'

She gave a little self-deprecating shrug. 'That's what I'm here for. Where are we going next?'

'To the pub,' I replied nervously. 'I don't really want to face Ted Harland again given how hostile he was earlier, but I do want to know if he knows anything about a will.'

'I shall come with you.' She patted my hand. 'Don't worry, dear. By ourselves we are simply two housewives but together we are completely formidable.'

I wasn't sure about that but I certainly felt a lot stronger and capable with Maud at my side.

The pub was unusually quiet for a Saturday afternoon. A sombre mood had settled over the village but Stan's death had clearly not put some of the men off their afternoon pints.

Mavis, the barmaid, looked at me with sympathy. 'I'm very

sorry, Mrs Miller. I heard the news. What a terrible shock it must have been.'

'Yes, it was. A quite terrible shock.'

'What can I get you?'

'Two lemonades, dear,' Maud said. 'And if you can let us know where we can find the two brothers who were staying here with Mr Miller, that would be very helpful.'

'They're in the snug,' she whispered, jerking her head towards a small room at the back of the pub. 'The older one, Ted, seems to be taking the death of his friend very hard.'

'Are they alone?'

Mavis placed our drinks on the bar and Maud paid her before I could get my purse out first. 'There's a couple of the regulars in there playing dominoes but so far as I can tell, both groups are keeping to themselves.'

I thanked her and we made our way to the snug with our lemonades. Ted Harland was slumped at a small table, an empty glass in front of him. Bernard sat opposite, nursing a half-pint of beer. He looked up as Maud and I entered, his expression unreadable.

'Mrs Miller,' Bernard said, rising politely. 'You and your friend are welcome to join us.'

'Thank you.' Maud and I took seats around the same table. 'I hope we're not intruding.'

'It is no intrusion,' he said smoothly. 'I'm sure we are all grieving in our own way.'

Ted didn't look up. He just stared into his empty glass. 'Grieving?' he slurred, his voice thick with emotion and drink. 'She's not grieving for Stan. For all we know, she probably killed him.'

'Ted, that's enough,' Bernard said sharply, placing a restraining hand on his brother's arm. 'We know you're upset, but that's no reason to accuse Mrs Miller of wrongdoing.'

'I'm sorry you have lost your good friend,' I said, ignoring Ted's accusation. 'But I can assure you, it wasn't me who killed him. I can't deny that I was very angry when he left Westleham without a word, especially because it left me short of money. However, Stan has been very fair with me since he returned. He was transferring the house over to me which would give me a good deal of security in the future, as I'm sure you can appreciate.'

'Please see this from Mrs Miller's point of view,' Maud beseeched Ted. 'She has received no money from her estranged husband during their time apart. Now he has passed on, she has no idea whether or not he made a will. This is crucially important because, if he did, the house she lives in could very soon be owned by someone else.'

'Stan wouldn't have done that,' Ted said.

'You sound very sure of that,' I replied.

'I'm positive.' Ted held his glass up.

'Don't you think you've had enough?' Bernard asked, his voice quiet and respectful, but I could still hear the slight note of panic in his voice.

'I'll decide when I've had enough.' Ted passed his glass to his brother. 'Get me another one, please.'

Despite his obvious reluctance, Bernard got to his feet and walked over to the bar.

'Why are you so sure?' I asked.

'Stan had come back to Westleham to put things right. He wanted to finalise things with you, with the house, and also with Walter Preston.'

'Walter Preston?' I asked in surprise. I couldn't imagine what business Stan would have with Walter Preston. Mr Preston was a businessman who was fairly new to the village. Rumour had it he was ruthless and some of his dealings did not fall on the right side of legal. It didn't seem likely to me that a man as strait-laced as Stan would have anything to do with a man like Walter Preston.

'Stan had dealings with him directly before he left.' Ted eyed me with pain-filled eyes. 'If you must know, Walter Preston is the reason Stan left.'

'Really?' I frowned. 'I always thought he left because he didn't love me.'

'He didn't.' Ted shrugged at Maud's sharp intake of breath. 'There's no point pretending otherwise. But the truth is, Stan left because Walter blackmailed him into doing something that made him deeply uncomfortable. It's pointless asking me what Walter had over Stan because he refused to tell me when I asked.'

'I can't imagine Stan doing something illegal,' I said doubtfully, still stung from the harsh reality of Ted's words. I couldn't, of course, deny the truth in them, but spoken out loud they were hard to hear.

'No.' Ted smiled as if remembering how very much a stickler Stan had been for doing things properly. 'He didn't commit a crime but all decent people would call what he did thoroughly rotten.'

'Will you tell me what he did?'

Bernard put a fresh pint in front of Ted, who took a sip before continuing. 'I'm not sure what you know about the housing market after the war?'

'Not much,' I said with a little embarrassment. 'I'm afraid I am quite closeted from a lot of things here in Westleham.'

'Not at all.' Ted shook his head. 'It was here in Westleham that the acts occurred. After the war, many families struggled financially. Sometimes it was because men didn't return, sometimes because they returned but were unable to work afterwards

– but lots of families with mortgages on their homes were in real danger of losing them.'

I felt a little breathless as Ted told his story. Somehow, the telling of it seemed to have sobered him up. 'That's terrible. Those poor families.'

'Stan, as you know, worked at a bank in the city. Part of his role meant that he could access the bank details of whomever he liked.'

'Is that wrong?'

'It is if he had no professional reason to be doing so.'

I was beginning to see the conclusion of Ted's narrative. 'And Stan didn't?'

'He didn't,' Ted confirmed. 'He found out which of his neighbours here in the village were struggling, then passed that information on to Walter Preston.'

'And that weasel swooped in and bought people's homes for a song, didn't he?' Maud asked angrily.

'Yes.' Ted looked down at the table, as though he was the one responsible for the shameful act. 'Preston approached the families and negotiated the sale of their home to him for far less than the market value.'

'That's not just rotten,' I said, 'it's completely unethical. Why would Stan do such a thing? That sort of behaviour is simply not in his nature.'

I wondered about Ted's earlier words about Walter blackmailing Stan. That had to be true – it was the only explanation for Stan to have behaved in such a manner.

'For the reason I've already stated,' Ted said sadly. 'He was being blackmailed, though what Walter Preston had over Stan, I don't know.'

'If the village were aware of this, Mr Preston would be ruined socially,' Maud said.

'Perhaps also financially if Stan followed through on his decision to notify the bank what he had done.'

'That's what you meant when you said Stan was coming back to put things right.'

'Yes.' Ted took a large swallow of his beer. 'Stan was sorry for the things he had done before leaving Westleham and wanted to come back and make things as right as he could before leaving for good.'

'That's why you think he wouldn't have left a will in someone else's favour?'

'I'm as sure as I can be that there is no will, Mrs Miller. Everything Stan owned will soon be yours. That makes you a very wealthy woman.'

'Does it?' I asked in complete shock.

'I think Stan told you he had some good fortune with his investments?'

'He did, but I must confess I don't understand stocks and shares or bonds – those sort of financial matters are beyond me.'

'You don't need to understand them but you may need some advice on reinvestment given there's such a large sum.'

It took a moment for the second shock to register; then its implications struck me like a body-blow. 'I shall certainly be the police's principal suspect when they discover how I stand to financially benefit.'

Even saying the words out loud felt odd. Me – a wealthy woman? Not for the first time since Stan's return, I felt as though I was living between the pages of a rather far-fetched novel.

'Maybe not the principal suspect,' Bernard interjected. 'Tell Mrs Miller the rest.'

'Stan said much of his life in Westleham was built on a series of small dishonesties, and he couldn't move on until he'd wiped the slate clean. He spoke to you yesterday morning, then tried to deal with Beckwith.' He stabbed a finger on the table for emphasis. 'And the night before he died, he went to see Walter Preston.'

'Thank you for sharing that with me,' I said in a voice I knew was more than a little prim. It was very difficult discussing Stan with someone who so obviously knew him much better than I ever had. 'We'll leave you now, but I'm very grateful for your honesty.'

As we stood up to leave, Bernard reached up and put a restraining hand on my arm. 'Be careful, Mrs Miller.'

I walked out of the pub with Maud in a daze. The longer the day went on, the larger the web of secrets Stan had left behind. He had returned to Westleham seeking redemption, but instead, he had found death. And I was beginning to see that in his quest to put his own past right, he had threatened to unravel the carefully constructed lives of too many people. One of whom surely must be his murderer.

7

'Well,' Maud said, her eyebrows raised so far it was almost comical. 'That was rather a turn up, wasn't it?'

'The news about Walter Preston was certainly unexpected.'

'Nonsense.' Maud looked at me as though I had lost my mind. 'That was the least unexpected thing that Ted said. That man always did give me the shivers. All smiles and handshakes, like a greengrocer weighing the apples with his thumb on the scale.'

'I think we should pay him a visit.'

'I was rather hoping you'd say that.' She set her shoulders, and we walked together towards The Limes, Walter Preston's handsome house on the lane leading out towards Farmer Bennington's fields.

The Limes had been a modest place when the Carters had lived there, before the war. Walter's improvements were evident even from the gate. The house, and windowsills, were freshly painted, a pair of stone urns flanked the tiled doorstep, and the brass door knocker gleamed in the weak afternoon sun.

When I lifted the knocker, the door opened almost at once, as though the owner had been either expecting our visit, or had watched our arrival.

Walter Preston stood there, immaculate in an open-necked shirt and waistcoat, his hair smoothed back, his expression set in polite concern.

'Mrs Miller. Mrs Burnett.' He stepped back neatly. 'What brings you both here on such a sad day? Won't you both come inside?'

We walked into a bright hall with a glass-fronted case of porcelain dogs and a smell of beeswax and pipe tobacco. He led us down the hall and into a sitting room where everything seemed newly upholstered and self-consciously tasteful.

'Tea?' he offered. 'Or something stronger? I keep a decent whisky.'

'No, thank you,' I said. 'We won't take up much of your time.'

'I am at your disposal,' he said, and the smile tightened. 'Please, make yourselves comfortable.'

We did as he suggested, but I had rarely felt so ill at ease in my life. How did one ask a man if they were an immoral chancer who had taken advantage of good people at the lowest point in their lives? Not to mention blackmailed a bank employee for his own gain.

I picked the easiest of the questions I wanted to ask. 'Did my husband call to speak with you last night?'

Walter folded his hands across his stomach, a glint I did not like flashing in his eyes. 'Yes, he did. His visit was rather unexpected and, if I may be blunt, not at all welcome.'

'I understand he wanted to put things right that he perceived he had done wrongly in the past.'

'That was the gist of it.' Walter shrugged. 'Quite why he thought I cared about the moralities of deals long put to bed, I've no idea.'

'Maybe he had a conscience?'

'Possibly, though as I've said, it was a little late to let it rule his decision-making.'

'Is it not a good thing to have peace of mind?'

'I can't say I've ever had a problem sleeping at night, and I don't think that is something that will ever be a problem for me.'

It seemed village talk about Walter Preston was right – what a thoroughly horrid man he was. That knowledge only made me more curious as to why Stan would have any dealings with such an unpleasant fellow.

'Did my husband help you to buy this house, as well as others, in the village?'

'I came here after the war hoping to settle in this charming little spot of the English countryside. An opportunity arose.' He gestured around him. 'I paid what was asked. Your husband made the introduction between me and the previous owners. There was nothing illegal in it.'

Maud snorted softly. 'Not illegal and not right are cousins, Mr Preston.'

His jaw tightened. 'Be that as it may, but according to the law, I have done nothing wrong.'

'You profited because the Carters couldn't afford their house after their two sons didn't return home from the war and Mr Carter, no doubt as a direct result, had a massive heart attack,' I said, outraged at his calm dismissal of his actions. 'Getting this house cheaply meant you had more money to spend on similar purchases.'

'You profited on the back of other people's misery.' Maud stared at Walter Preston contemptuously.

'Did you argue with Stan?' I asked.

'Your husband was overwrought, Mrs Miller. I simply told

him that if he wished to air old business, he should do so sensibly.'

'Did he do as you suggested?'

Walter's mouth twisted into a wry smile. 'Alas, no. He had the temerity to suggest we recompense the Carters – and other families – out of our own pockets. I told him at once such a proposal was madness and that I would have no part of it.'

'So he was trying to right past wrongs?' I couldn't help admiring Stan's attempts to do the right thing no matter the personal cost to himself. It made me feel sad that I would never have the chance to tell him that I was proud of him for standing up to Walter Preston.

'Ridiculous,' Walter scoffed. 'It's pointless locking the stable door after the horse has already bolted.'

'What I don't understand is why he would do such a thing in the first place.'

'He took some persuasion.' A particularly nasty smile played across his lips and made the man look positively evil. 'I could tell you how I convinced him but I don't think your sensibilities could cope with such a revelation.'

I leaned forward, eager to get the truth out of him, but Maud placed a restraining hand on my arm. 'I don't think that information is pertinent to our visit.'

Maud's words made me pause and remember the reason I was there. It wasn't to find out what had happened in the past, it was to try and uncover Stan's murderer.

'Of course, you're right,' I said to Maud before turning back to Walter. 'Did you come to the village green this morning to watch the cricket match?'

'Of course,' he said at once, and then paused. 'That is to say, I walked round after breakfast. Everyone did. Flags, bunting, village lads knocking a ball about... It was the first bit of cheer we've had in an age. A pity how it ended.'

'Did you stay to watch the match or talk to any of the players in the pavilion?' I asked.

He glanced at me sharply. 'I watched the match but had no reason to go into the pavilion. The action was on the field, not in that awful wooden structure.'

I stood – I couldn't stand to be in the odious man's presence for any longer than was necessary. 'Thank you for your time, Mr Preston.'

'If you'll take a gentleman's advice, Mrs Miller, your husband wanted to stir up old business dealings. It's probably best you don't do the same. Best to let things lie.'

I didn't respond, but his words bothered me – was I being threatened? Walter's face was impassive as he spoke but I couldn't help but think he was pointing out Stan had died after trying to put things right, and the same might happen to me.

As I stepped out of the house, and back into the garden, something I had missed on my arrival caught my eye. One of the borders to the left of the path had been recently dug; the soil still showed the marks of a fork. Among the geraniums, a little clutch of leaves had pushed up – glossy, dark green, and deeply divided into lobes. The plant was not yet in bloom but it was unmistakable once one knew it.

'Pretty border,' I remarked.

Walter followed my gaze. 'The garden was a dreadful mess when I bought the house. With some help from a young lad from the village, I've been improving it. He says I've the sort of soil that will grow anything.'

'Indeed,' I said, and suppressed the shiver that went through me. Monkshood without its blue cloaks is only a plant to those who don't know it. To those who do, it is a quiet, dangerous thing and has no business in the borders of a household garden.

We walked away, and when we reached the lane, Maud let out a breath she had been holding. 'Why did you mention that plant?'

'It grows all over. In hedge-bottoms. I've seen it in the graveyard and down by Lovers' Leap. It proves nothing, of course.' I rubbed my gloved hand unconsciously. 'But that's monkshood, the plant I think may have been used to poison Stan.'

'Well if that's definitely the poison, he certainly had easy access to it,' Maud observed as we reached the garden gate. 'I presume you want to go to the farm and speak to young Frank?'

'Yes, he's been the one tending Walter Preston's garden. So like that horrible man not to know his name, or that he lives on the farm. How rude to just call him "a young lad".'

'Did you think his comment about letting things lie was a warning?'

I shivered and pulled my cardigan closer around my shoulders, though not because I was cold. 'It could have been a simple throwaway comment, just like Bernard Harland's was, but equally they both could have been veiled threats.'

'The sort of man who would take advantage of grieving families wouldn't hesitate to silence someone threatening to expose him.' Maud caught hold of my arm, and I stopped walking to face her. 'You know, I would feel a lot happier if you would put that cheque Oliver Beckwith gave you into your handbag. If it comes out of your pocket and flies over the farmer's fields, I for one am not going chase across them and help you retrieve it.'

I unclasped my handbag, took the carefully folded cheque from my pocket and tucked it away. 'You're right, of course. I don't know why I did that.'

But I did know.

I'd put it with Luke's letter. In some corner of my mind the two items seemed intrinsically linked: a promise of money, and the promise of Luke.

'If I'm not mistaken, that cheque was for a very nice sum of money,' Maud commented as innocently as she was able. However, I knew she actually meant it as a question and was eagerly waiting for my answer.

'It is,' I agreed and hid a smile at Maud's look of annoyance.

As we reached the farm, Ada appeared in the doorway of the farmhouse, wiping her hands on her apron, her face brightening when she saw us.

'Martha, Maud!' Her expression changed from happiness at seeing us to one of concern. 'Martha, I'm so sorry about this morning. What a dreadful thing to happen.'

'Thank you, Ada. It's been a very strange day, to say the least.' Ada stood back and led us into the farmhouse kitchen. 'Now, what can I do for you? I know you well enough to be aware you haven't walked out here for a friendly chat.'

'We're hoping to talk to Frank,' I said.

Ada lowered her voice. 'Oh, my goodness, has Luke found out about Frank and Iris?'

'No, nothing like that,' I assured her. 'Though, I may mention it, just so he's aware.'

'Please don't mention my name,' Ada said. 'It can be quite tricky being a stepmother, I wouldn't want Frank to think I'm a blabbermouth.'

'Of course not.' I smiled. 'It makes it much easier to mention given Ruby saw the two of them this morning.'

'Oh, yes, that does keep me out of it. Now, if you haven't come to talk to Frank about that, what do you want to discuss with him?'

'Am I right in thinking Frank has been working on Walter Preston's garden?'

'Yes, that's right.' Ada nodded. 'Frank says he would stop doing it because the man is ever so particular, but apparently he pays well.'

'Oh, another thing, while I remember,' I said. 'Do you happen to know who keeps the keys for the pavilion? I know John was the scorer, so I thought he may know.'

'John himself,' Ada said with a note of pride in her new husband that was hard to miss. 'He went early to open the pavilion and get the scoreboard out and the numbers ready.'

'Are John and Frank about?'

'It's nearly three so they'll be back for their afternoon cup of tea any minute. We can all have a cup of tea together while you chat. Unless, of course, your conversation is private?'

'That sounds wonderful,' I said.

While the kettle boiled, and we waited for the men to return to the farmhouse, I filled Ada in on all she had missed since Stan's death.

'That's one thing I miss about being in the village,' Ada said. 'I miss what's going on. By the time we hear about things here at the farm, it's hours after the event has happened.'

'How are things, Ada?' Maud asked. 'You certainly look very happy.'

Ada beamed. 'I'm so busy these days, but in a good way. Looking after a big family is all I ever wanted, so I feel blessed. You never know, I might be blessed further, and our family may even expand more.'

'Ada!' Maud said sharply and stared deeply at our friend. 'Do you have something to tell us?'

Ada turned to the stove to remove the whistling kettle, but

not quickly enough to hide her flushed cheeks. 'Not yet. But if I do, you will be the first to know after John and the children.'

She wrapped a dishcloth around the handle of the kettle and carried it over to the table. I examined her as she did so, searching for any little sign that might show that Ada was expecting a baby. I couldn't see anything, but then again, my only knowledge of childbearing was my mother's multiple pregnancies. The first sign a sibling was due was my mother rushing to the outside lavatory in a morning.

'I think I need to visit Mrs Taylor's haberdashery shop and buy more wool,' Maud declared, then, seeing Ada's face, added, 'Just in case, of course.'

'Let's change the subject before the men get in,' Ada pleaded. 'Who's your prime suspect, Martha?'

'At present, Oliver Beckwith and Walter Preston look the likeliest. But I wouldn't dismiss either of the Harland brothers. Then there's Lavinia Thompson, she was very upset when she heard Stan dismissing their relationship. And I would be remiss if I didn't consider Luke.'

'Luke?' Ada's voice was stunned. 'Surely not.'

I lifted a shoulder in a slight shrug. 'He wants us to be together. Last night he even mentioned to me that he was thinking of leaving the Church.'

'Goodness,' Ada said. 'That would be a big decision.'

'And it's a little coincidental that the very next day Stan is killed,' I said miserably. 'It's not something I want to contemplate but equally, I can't rule it out. Especially because one of the places where I know monkshood grows is the graveyard.'

We fell silent as heavy boots sounded on the path outside the kitchen. Moments later, John, Frank, and another two Bennington boys came in after shedding their boots.

'Good afternoon, ladies,' John said heartily, then walked over and kissed his wife's cheek. 'Hello, dear.'

To my surprise, Ada flushed again. She had never seemed the sort of woman to allow romance to fluster her but here she was acting as giddily as a teenaged girl. It was a rather delightful sight and I was so happy for my friend that her whirlwind romance, which originally started as a convenient arrangement for Ada and John, had blossomed into something much more.

'Hello, Mrs Burnett.' Frank nodded at my neighbour. 'Sleuthing again, Mrs Miller?'

I nodded. 'That's right, Frank. I wonder if you can answer a few questions for me?'

'Me?' Frank looked doubtful. 'I wouldn't have thought I'll be any use to you. The only time I met your husband was this morning directly before the game started.'

I looked at John. 'Did you have the keys for the pavilion?'

'Yes, that's right. Me and the boys went down early to open up and get the scoreboard out. Frank was opening the batting with Luke so needed to have his pads on ready.'

'And was the pavilion left open during Westleham's batting?'

'Yes, it was.' John frowned at my question but continued. 'It needed to be open so that each new batsman had time to go in and change before it was their turn to bat. Equally those who were out could go in and take off their pads.'

'So anyone could have gone in at any time during the morning?'

'Yes, anyone. Why, is there a problem with the pavilion?'

I shook my head. 'Not with the pavilion, but perhaps with Stan's kit. We'll know more later, but thank you for clarifying that for me.'

'Now, young man,' Maud said, addressing Frank. 'What can you tell us about your duties with Mr Preston's garden?'

'He's the most infuriating man,' Frank said. 'He insisted he wanted his geraniums planted out. Everyone knows you wait until the end of the month, but he insisted he wanted them planting. He's certain to blame me if they die.'

Ada quietly passed cups of tea around the table. 'What about the monkshead?'

'Well, that was really odd.' Frank added so much sugar to his tea, I couldn't help but wonder if his entire weekly allowance had gone into that one cup. 'He wanted it planting in and around the geranium. He thought the purple flowers of the monkshead would look good next to the pink geraniums.'

'Did you explain to him how poisonous it is?'

'Oh yes.' Frank nodded. 'He told me to make sure I brought gloves from home and wore them while working. Can you believe he didn't want me to touch poisonous plants with his gardening gloves. He really is insufferable, but he does pay rather well.'

'Let me get this straight,' I said. 'He deliberately wanted monkshood planting in his front garden despite knowing how deadly it is.'

'That's right.' Frank took a sip of tea. 'He told me he had seen this lovely plant in the churchyard and described it to me. Of course, I knew what it was, and explained that to him. He wanted some taking from the churchyard and replanting in his garden.'

'That's extremely peculiar.'

'Mr Preston even got me to ask the vicar if it was all right to uproot some of the monkshood in the churchyard.'

My heart hammered so loudly, I was sure everyone in the kitchen could hear it. 'So the vicar knew it was there?'

'I'm not sure if he knew before I asked to take some.'

'What did he say?'

'When I told him how deadly it was, he said I was welcome to dig up as much of it as I liked.'

I almost wished I hadn't asked the question. Although I now knew Walter Preston had specifically asked for monkshood to be planted in his garden, I was also aware that Luke not only knew where it grew but also that it was poisonous.

'You'd best watch yourself, Frank!' One of his brothers, I forget his name, poked Frank in the ribs. 'If the vicar catches you with his sister, you might be the next one to get bumped off!'

'Jack!' John thundered. 'Apologise to Mrs Miller immediately.'

Jack's face turned redder than the village telephone box. 'Oh, Mrs Miller, I'm so sorry. I didn't think.'

'Don't worry, Jack, you haven't upset me.'

But he had.

Not for the reason he thought, though, but because Jack had suggested Luke as a murderer. I knew he was making a joke at his brother's expense but even so, I couldn't help but worry that other people would jump to the same conclusion if I was right and monkshood turned out to be the poison that had killed Stan.

8

We walked in silence past the village green, where the abandoned cricket stumps stood as a stark reminder of the morning's tragedy. The bunting that had seemed so cheerful hours before now hung limp in the soft evening breeze.

I was looking forward to sitting in my house, gathering my thoughts, and enjoying some peace and quiet. The day's events had been extremely trying.

'Stop brooding, Martha,' Maud said. 'I know what you're thinking, but you're wrong. Just because Jack made a joke about Luke it doesn't mean he, or anyone else, actually thinks Luke capable of murder.'

'But what if—'

Maud stopped walking and turned to face me. 'Martha, you must stop torturing yourself with suspicions about that man. Everything we've learned about him during his time here in Westleham points away from him, not towards him.'

'Does it?' I asked. 'He knew about the monkshood in the churchyard and had easy access to the pavilion and every reason to want Stan out of our lives.'

'Luke was first in bat,' Maud pointed out. 'Which means it's highly unlikely he had a chance to put monkshood in Stan's glove.'

I sighed deeply. 'You're right, of course. I'm letting my fears cloud my judgement.'

'Your fears?'

I looked down at the road. 'I'm afraid that if Luke is guilty, it means he killed Stan for me. And if he did that...' I trailed off, unable to voice the terrible thought.

'If he did that, then he's not the man you thought he was,' Maud finished gently. 'But Martha, nothing we've learned today suggests that's the case. You know, a wise woman once said: don't borrow trouble, it charges terrible interest.'

'Was that wise woman you?' I smiled appreciatively at my friend.

'Why yes. Yes, it was.'

'You're a good friend,' I told her.

'We need to find out more facts,' she said decisively, smiling at my compliment, but continuing her staunch defence of Luke. 'Facts that will prove his innocence.'

'Or prove his guilt.' I couldn't help adding. 'The question is how do I go about investigating the man I—' I stopped myself before I could say 'love'. It felt wrong to speak of my strong feelings for Luke when Stan was barely cold.

Maud looked around at the fields and empty lane. 'It's all right, Martha. There's no one here to hear you. I have two eyes in my head and am well aware of how you two feel about each other. The next few days won't be easy, I'm sure, but if he's innocent, which I'm certain he is, the truth will bear that out. And if he's not – well, it's better to know now than later.'

I nodded; I really was so lucky to have such a wise woman as both friend and neighbour. As we approached the village, I could see two people waiting at my garden gate. 'Oh, who is that?'

Maud peered into the distance at the two women. 'It looks as though it's your friend Annie and that soppy woman Lavinia Thompson.'

'I suppose I'm going to have to invite them in,' I said with regret. 'I'd really rather just be alone for a little while. No offence, Maud, I've appreciated your company this afternoon, but I could do with a chance to think about the things we've learned.'

'Oh, Martha! I'm so glad you're back,' Annie called excitedly as we approached. 'Your sister said you'd be along. Lavinia has something to tell you of great importance. Her information might be crucial to your investigation. Oh, do please tell me that you are investigating.'

'I am indeed,' I confirmed. 'You'd better both come inside.'

I led my guests to the kitchen and wearily filled the kettle before setting it on the stove. As I picked up a box of matches, Annie stopped me.

'Oh, Martha, don't worry about tea for us unless you're making it for yourself and Mrs Burnett. We've just had the most delightful afternoon tea at the Cricketer's Arms.'

I smiled. Winnie Noble was quite the snob, but passing off a few sandwiches, a slice of cake, and a pot of tea as 'afternoon tea' – as if the Cricketer's Arms were the Ritz – was rather impressive.

I joined the other women who were already sitting around my kitchen table. Lavinia positively vibrated with excitement, though her eyes were red-rimmed. I doubted the tears she cried at Stan's dismissal of their relationship were the only ones she had cried that day. It disturbed me a little to think that she had probably shed more tears for Stan than I had.

She was a neat woman with immaculately styled hair and

pale hands that showed the faint, stubborn stains of the dyes she used for her sewing.

'How wonderful,' I said to Annie, then turned to Lavinia. 'Now, do tell me, Miss Thompson, what information do you have to share with me?'

'I was struggling to sleep last night,' she began. 'I thought perhaps if I went for a little walk around the village, it might help me to sleep. Instead of being soothing, it made it even harder for me to settle.'

'Did you see something you perhaps shouldn't have?'

'I heard voices near the pavilion,' she said, looking around as though to make sure she had a captive audience before continuing. 'I was about to turn back to the pub when I heard two men talking. It was very wrong of me, I know, but I couldn't help myself. I crept closer so I could hear them more clearly.'

'Lavinia!' Annie said in surprise. 'That isn't at all like you.'

'I know.' She bowed her head, like a child before a schoolmistress. 'I was certain that one of the men was Stan.'

'Of course, you would know his voice.' I kept my voice neutral but was surprised how difficult it was. Our marriage had been far from perfect, but I was a little perturbed that Lavinia was so brazen in her admiration for my husband. 'Did you recognise the other man?'

'I've heard him talk at the pub a few times these last couple of days so after a few moments of listening to their conversation, I was confident the other man was the younger Harland brother. Bernard, I believe his name is.'

It surprised me that Stan had been meeting Bernard in secret. From what I had understood, it was Stan and Ted who were friends. Bernard was simply Ted's brother and therefore a friend by extension. 'Could you hear exactly what they were talking about?'

'Not every word,' Lavinia admitted. 'But enough for me to catch the gist.'

My breath caught. This could be significant indeed. 'What were they talking about?'

'I didn't understand it at first,' she said. 'Stan was asking Bernard if he had thought about what they discussed and how if he didn't stop what he was doing when they went back to Brighton, he would tell Ted what Bernard had been doing.'

'Did you hear what Stan was accusing Bernard of doing?'

Lavinia nodded, trembling with excitement. 'He was selling prescription-only medicines for cash.'

'How on earth was he doing that?' I wondered. And why? Ted was clearly rather well off so it seemed strange that his brother needed to raise extra money – particularly by carrying out a fraudulent scheme. Bernard had seemed such a clean-cut man but, of course, I already knew from bitter experience that people were very rarely exactly what they seemed.

'From what I could gather, he has a forged prescription pad and has been fabricating a doctor's signature.' She shook her head sadly. 'It was all very unsavoury.'

'That's dreadful.' I could understand now why Lavinia had seemed so giddy about what she had overheard.

'Stan sounded outraged,' Lavinia said in a proud voice. 'He told Bernard in no uncertain terms that if he didn't promise to stop, he would report him. Bernard then said that just because Stan was putting right his own wrongs, that didn't mean he should interfere with his dealings.'

I could well imagine Stan being angry with Bernard. From what we had learned, Stan's own immoral actions had been carried out as a result of blackmail. Bernard was moving higher up my suspect list. He had good reason to make sure Stan didn't tell anyone what he had been doing.

'What a despicable thing to do,' Maud commented.

'Then Mr Harland said something that chilled me to the bone.' Lavinia paused dramatically. 'He said, "If your conscience is so important to you, Stan, I hope you are ready for the consequences of your interference."'

Annie gasped. 'Well, that's a clear threat.'

'Have you told the police?' I asked.

'Not yet,' Lavinia admitted. 'I wanted to tell you first and make sure you thought what I had heard would be important to the police.'

I raised an eyebrow. 'Really? Surely you knew straight away that it was something that should be reported. If not immediately, then certainly after Stan's death.'

Lavinia's composure crumbled and she began to weep into a neat, white handkerchief. 'Because I'm a foolish woman. Forgive me, Mrs Miller, but even after all these years I harboured feelings for Stan. When he made those remarks this morning, and I realised how little I had meant to him, I was so hurt and angry that I actually wanted him to suffer but I never thought for a minute that Bernard would actually kill Stan.'

I reached over and patted her hand. 'You've done the right thing by telling us now.'

She looked at me through her tears. 'I was going to warn him to be careful this morning. Then I overheard those cruel words and I realised he had never loved me the way I loved him. Oh, I feel so foolish.'

Soon after Lavinia's revelation, Annie made their excuses and they got up to leave. I saw them to the front door. As Annie walked down the path towards my garden gate, Lavinia turned and caught my arm. 'Mrs Miller, I hope you can forgive me for not speaking sooner. And I hope that you know that despite everything that happened between Stan and me years ago, and what he said this morning, I would never wish him any harm. He was a genuinely good man.'

'I know,' I replied, surprised that I meant exactly what I said – I would not have said the same thing only a few days ago. 'Thank you for coming forward and sharing what you know.'

'I hope it helps in uncovering the murderer,' she said. 'I will go and tell the police what I've told you.'

As I closed the door behind her, I reflected on how much my life had changed in a single day. This morning, I had been a wife – unhappy, but still bound by the ties of marriage. Now I was a widow, and very possibly a wealthy one if Ted Harland was correct about both Stan's investments and the fact that he had not left a will.

* * *

An hour or so later, I was sitting in the parlour listening to the radio when there was yet another knock at the front door. Maud had gone home, and Ruby was in her room. I thought seriously about not answering, not certain I could cope with anything more that day.

I counted to ten, then wearily got to my feet and went to the door. I pulled back my shoulders and took a deep breath before answering.

'Good evening, Mrs Miller,' Ben said solemnly. 'May we come in?'

A tall, middle-aged man with an extremely earnest expression stood at Ben's side. He offered me his hand. 'Detective Inspector Alan Kennington. I've taken over the inquiry into your husband's death.'

I shook his hand and stepped back from the door to let them in. 'It's nice to meet you. Can I get either of you tea?'

'No, thank you. I'd like to let you know where we are with the case before we continue questioning our suspects.' He exchanged a glance with Ben as he emphasised 'our' – it was a mild rebuke, and I wondered if he might follow it with a more pointed warning about staying out of police business.

Leading them through to the parlour, I took my favourite seat next to the window and turned off the radio. 'Please make yourselves comfortable.'

Ben sat on the sofa, but his colleague remained on his feet. 'I'm afraid to say that we have received word from the mortuary that your husband's death is likely a murder.'

Of course, I had already come to that conclusion, but hearing it out loud from the investigating officer still felt like a physical blow. 'Have they… that is… the mortuary—'

'The pathologist has not yet commenced the post-mortem.' Detective Inspector Kennington correctly guessed what I had not been able to put into words. 'That is scheduled for tomorrow morning. Neither have they completed the tests on Mr Miller's cricket glove. However, from Mr Walker's evidence, and from the condition of Mr Miller's body, I have been given an initial opinion of death by poisoning – the poison likely being monkshood.'

It felt strange hearing Luke referred to as Mr Walker. He was so often just called 'vicar' by the entire village that I had almost forgotten he even had a surname. 'I see,' I said lamely.

'Of course that opinion is subject to confirmation by the pathologist when he has completed the post-mortem and received all test results. I wanted to come and let you know the up-to-date information as we have it, as well as introduce myself.'

'I appreciate that,' I said, even though the detective had not told me anything I hadn't already worked out for myself.

'Now, Mrs Miller.' Detective Inspector Kennington rocked

gently on his heels, as though he had trouble keeping still. 'I'm afraid that I must ask you some direct questions about your husband's return and the circumstances surrounding his death.'

'Of course,' I said, though my stomach clenched with apprehension. I knew I hadn't done anything wrong, but I was certain my face had flushed. Licking my suddenly dry lips, I tried not to look guilty under his intense scrutiny. 'How may I help?'

'Were you aware that your husband had returned to Westleham to, shall we say, settle old scores?'

'I learned yesterday and today that Stan felt he had some wrongs to right, yes. But he didn't confide the specifics to me other than how it affected me directly.'

'And how did it affect you?'

'Stan told me yesterday morning that he intended to transfer the house into my name. During our discussion, it became clear to him that the money he had arranged to be sent to me by the village solicitor, Oliver Beckwith, had not been received by me. I'm aware that he later had a discussion with Mr Beckwith about this matter, which led to a minor altercation.'

He nodded. 'I have received Mr Beckwith's complaint.'

'You should be aware that I spoke to the solicitor today and he gave me a cheque for the missing money.' I lifted my handbag onto my knee. 'I have it here, if you need to see it?'

He shook his head. 'That will not be necessary. I'm glad the money has been returned to you. Naturally, however, we will be looking into why that hasn't happened over the past couple of years.'

'I see.'

The detective looked down at his notebook. 'You carried your husband's cricket equipment over to the cricket ground this morning?'

'I did,' I confirmed. 'It had been stored in his bedroom and he left a message with Ruby, my sister, asking me to bring it over for the start of the match.'

'For how long had it been in the bedroom?' He frowned as he made a note. 'And where, precisely, had it been kept?'

I gave a small shrug. 'I presume since we moved into the house. It was in his wardrobe.'

'My apologies for the indelicacy of my next question.' For the first time since his arrival, the detective looked uncomfortable. 'You said his bedroom. Were you not in the habit of sharing a room with your husband?'

'We were not,' I said, lifting my chin proudly, though inside, the shame of talking about our marriage was mortifying. 'After our marriage, and moving into this house, I had my room and Stan had his. Whilst he occasionally came into my room, I very rarely went into his. However, when I put away his clean clothes, I was aware of the cricket equipment in the wardrobe.'

'Thank you for confirming that. Is it possible to speak with your sister to confirm that Mr Miller asked you to bring the equipment over with you?'

'Yes.' I made to stand, but the detective raised a hand.

'Not just yet. I will speak to her after I have finished with you.' It was impossible not to feel concerned at the thorough interrogation. 'Did your sister know where the cricket equipment was kept?'

'I shouldn't have thought so,' I said. 'Perhaps Stan told her when he came to the house, but Ruby wouldn't have done anything Stan asked without checking with me first.'

'But it wasn't hidden?' he pressed. 'Anyone who came into the house could have looked around, found the cricket gloves, and tampered with them.'

'I suppose so,' I admitted. 'Though, of course, it's much more likely that the poison was put into the glove in the pavilion.'

He gave me a long, speculative look. 'Is that so?'

'How would the killer have known Stan's equipment was even here in the house?' I asked. 'It's much more likely that the killer went into the pavilion. Especially because Stan was the last batsman. They had plenty of time to go in undetected whereas the chances of being discovered coming either into or out of my house would be high.'

Detective Inspector Kennington made another note in his book. 'Were you aware of your husband's financial situation? His investments, for instance?'

'He said yesterday he'd done well and intended to pay off our mortgage and transfer the house to me.' I hesitated, then added, 'I've learned since his death that he may have been quite wealthy.'

'Indeed. Mr Harland has given us Mr Miller's personal effects. It's clear from his bank book that your husband had accumulated a considerable sum – enough to make his death extremely financially beneficial to you.'

The words were delivered coolly but the insinuation was clear. Ben shifted uncomfortably on the sofa.

'Detective Inspector,' I said as evenly as I could manage, 'if you're suggesting I killed my husband for money, I should point out that he was already transferring the house to me. Why would I risk murder when I was getting what I needed through legal means?'

'Perhaps because a house is considerably less than everything,' he replied with a raised eyebrow.

'I shall have to take your word for that.' I met his stare with one of my own. 'I knew nothing of my husband's financial affairs prior to his death.'

I wanted to say more, but thought that calmly stating the facts would be better than an over-emotional rant. The detective's appraisal of me was extremely unnerving but I was determined not to crack. After all, I had done nothing wrong.

Detective Inspector Kennington made another note, then closed his notebook with a sharp snap. 'Mrs Miller, I must caution you not to interfere with this investigation. I understand you've had some... involvement in previous cases, but this matter concerns your husband's death. We shall need to eliminate you from our enquiries.'

I couldn't help myself. 'I can only be a suspect if I stand to inherit Stan's estate and knew about his wealth. As things stand, I am a widow who could well be living in a house he's left to someone else, and as I've said, I knew nothing of his finances.'

'No one is excluded at this stage,' he replied, echoing Ben's earlier words. 'Your cooperation this afternoon is appreciated. We will be making enquiries with solicitors in Brighton with regard to Mr Miller's will so it would be premature of me to speculate on who will inherit his estate. However, all the information available to me at this stage suggests that Mr Miller did not make a will.'

I was glad to be sitting down; my head was spinning and a wave of dizziness swept over me. If two years as a deserted wife had seemed like something out of a fiction book, then the events of the past day were beyond all belief.

* * *

Lizzy's warm presence comforted me as I let her into the back garden for her nightly constitutional. The events of the day pressed heavily on my mind – Stan's death, the revelation about his wealth, the mounting evidence that made me look increasingly guilty.

Ruby had gone to bed, leaving me alone with my thoughts. I

leaned against the door jamb watching Lizzy explore the garden. Suddenly she stopped, a low growl rumbling the length of her body. Her hackles were raised, and she was staring intently at something in the shadows.

'What is it, girl?' I called softly. Of course, she didn't answer. Neither did she look my way, which was decidedly odd. 'Lizzy, come here.'

She didn't budge. The last time she had reacted in this way, she'd been protecting the garden from a hedgehog. Sighing, I walked over to her. Pinpricks of unease stabbed their way along my spine. Telling myself I was just on edge because of the terrible day I'd had, I forced myself to stay calm. The garden was bathed in shadows and I wished I'd taken the time to grab the torch I kept in the kitchen drawer.

'Lizzy!' I hissed.

She whined in response, but still did not move. I turned sharply at a noise to my left, then relaxed as I realised it was just the branches of the apple tree gently bobbing.

Looking back to Lizzy, I was about to call her again when I caught a definite movement in my peripheral vision.

Someone was in my garden!

'Who's there?'

My voice shook, my legs as wobbly as a newborn foal's. Perhaps instead of whispering into the night, I should just shout – that would either scare away whoever was prowling in my garden, or wake Ruby and Maud. My brain had just processed that thought when Lizzy sprung forward to stand next to me and the shadow became a person brandishing a large tree branch.

Lizzy barked frantically as I tried to back away from the intruder, but I was too slow. The thick branch swung towards me, cracking me on the side of the head.

I fell to the ground, the grass cool and a little damp against my cheek. Footsteps hurried out of the garden and around the side of the house. My vision blurred, and despite my best efforts, I couldn't lift my head.

Luke's face drifted through my consciousness like a particularly lovely dream before the effort of keeping my eyes open was too much and they fluttered closed.

9

I awoke to find myself lying on the grass in my back garden. Lizzy was whimpering pitifully at my side, Maud and Ruby hovering over me with worried looks on their faces. I tried to sit up.

Ruby, face pale in the light of the moon, knelt beside me. 'Don't try to sit up. I ran over the road to the vicarage. Luke has gone to fetch the doctor and the police. You mustn't move until Dr Briggs says you can.'

My head throbbed as though it were on the tracks and the 7.05 to London was hurtling towards me. A warm blanket lay over me and if it wasn't for the damp ground and my banging head, it might be quite nice out here under the stars.

Maud pointed at me, a stern look on her dear face. 'Martha Miller! Stop fidgeting right now. You are not to move until you are told it's safe.'

I reached up to touch my head. Ruby took hold of my hand and tucked it back underneath the cover. The wave of nausea that rushed through me at even that slight movement was enough to convince me I didn't need to touch my injury.

'Can you talk?' Ruby asked anxiously.

I closed my eyes and took in a slow, deep breath. 'Of course.'

'Oh thank goodness,' she breathed. 'I was worried that huge egg on your head might have caused permanent damage.'

My face felt warm, as though someone had trickled warm water over my skin. 'I feel extremely odd.'

'Well, you've got a tea towel on your head,' Maud said, in a matter-of-fact tone I was grateful for. 'It's like the tea towels the children wear when they act as shepherds in the school nativity – we tied it with one of Stan's old ties to stop the bleeding, you see. As Ruby has already said, you've got a large lump on your head, but we think that's the extent of your injuries.'

I tried to nod, to agree I wasn't hurt anywhere else, but quickly realised that was not a good idea. Any type of movement made the small amount of supper I'd consumed threaten to make a reappearance.

'How did you know I'd been attacked?'

'Lizzy,' Ruby said. 'She was barking loud enough to wake the entire village. Well, apart from you. She barked, whined, licked your face, but you didn't move. I don't mind telling you that Maud and I were extremely scared.'

She squeezed my hand, and I opened my eyes a fraction to share a smile with her. 'I'm all right.'

Footsteps hurrying down my garden path reminded me that the intruder had left the same way. I shouldn't think the police could get any usable fingerprints from my garden gate, but it was worth mentioning to them.

Within moments, four sets of eyes – Dr Briggs, Detective Inspector Kennington, Ben, and Luke – stared down at me.

'What happened?'

There was so much I wanted to say to Luke, but I couldn't say any of it while I was lying flat out in my back garden with what seemed like half the village listening in.

'I brought Lizzy out so she could do her business before bed,' I said. 'Someone was in the garden. I thought it was a hedgehog at first because Lizzy was growling. You know how she doesn't like them. When I walked over, whoever it was hit me with a large branch.'

'Did you recognise the person?' the detective asked.

Dr Briggs pushed his way past. 'Now, gentlemen, I understand you are concerned and have questions. However, I have yet to examine the patient and determine whether or not she is well enough to speak with you.'

'It was too dark,' I said quickly. 'All I saw was a shadow coming at me.'

'Now, Mrs Miller,' the doctor admonished. 'Lie still and let's take a look at you. That's an interestingly put-together bandage – your handiwork, I assume, Mrs Burnett?'

'Yes, Doctor.' The pride in Maud's voice made me smile.

I hated to think what I must look like with a tea towel fastened around my head by a tie, and blood running down my face. Thank goodness I hadn't changed for bed before bringing Lizzy outside. The only thing worse than my current predicament would have been if I was found in my nightwear.

Or, of course, death – but I refused to think about that as a real possibility. Surely no one would want me dead?

'Is the kettle on?' he asked.

'Of course, Doctor,' Maud answered as though she had been expecting his question. 'Plenty of water boiling in a large saucepan, too. I wasn't sure how much you would need. Clean towels are ready when you are.'

'She's had a blow to her head,' Ruby said. 'She's not having a baby.'

'I should think not,' Maud answered tartly. 'She's been as good as a single woman for the last two years!'

'Everyone inside!' the doctor demanded. 'No one here is having a baby. At least, not imminently.'

His remark confused me, but I didn't have the energy to ask him what he meant.

'I've got a torch,' the detective said. 'Shall I point it at Mrs Miller's injury so you can look at it?'

'Excellent idea,' Dr Briggs answered. 'The rest of you, get out of my way!'

With a good deal of shuffling feet, murmuring voices, and muttered complaints, those deemed superfluous by the doctor went inside.

Dr Briggs snapped open his bag and I closed my eyes again as the bright light from Detective Inspector Kennington's torch shone into my face. The doctor's fingers were gentle as he removed the temporary bandage and touched the area where I'd been hit.

'Will I need stitches?'

'I don't think so. There's a lot of blood but that's because the wound is high up in your hairline. Those types of injuries do bleed a lot, but it's not deep enough to need stitches. I'll check again and make sure once it's clean and we're inside with better lighting.'

'What can you tell me?' the detective asked Dr Briggs. 'Who could have done such a thing? Man, woman, young, old? Who am I looking for?'

I opened my eyes again to see the doctor pointing at something behind me. 'Anyone who can pick up that big branch and wield it.'

'You can't narrow down my suspect?' The disappointment in the detective's voice was evident. 'And neither can you, Mrs Miller?'

'All I can tell you is that it wasn't a tall man.'

'Not tall?' he pressed. 'What does that mean, exactly?'

'Taller than me – which isn't saying much, as I'm a short woman – but not as tall as the vicar.'

I might have been uncertain when talking to Maud earlier about Luke, but on this matter, I was positive. The person who attacked me was most definitely not Luke. Not only was the height of my assailant all wrong, but I knew with complete certainty that he would never do a single thing to harm me.

* * *

Ten minutes later, I had been helped by the doctor and the detective into my kitchen. My stomach still roiled as though I were on a small boat in the middle of a particularly vicious storm, but it wasn't as bad as when I'd first regained consciousness.

Dr Briggs insisted Detective Inspector Kennington wait in the parlour with everyone else while he cleaned and re-dressed my injury. I wasn't sure whether the detective, or Maud, was the most perturbed. Maud had clearly wanted to help the doctor tend to my wounds. The doctor, just as clearly, did not want any help.

I flinched as he parted my matted hair and frowned at the wound. 'It's a really nasty gash, Mrs Miller, but I think you'll manage without stitches. However, I don't recommend traipsing around the village for the next few days. You need complete rest.'

'But I must find out who killed Stan,' I protested.

'Leave that to the police,' he said quietly, looking at the closed kitchen door before continuing. 'Whoever killed Mr Miller did so in a particularly awful fashion. I wouldn't want whoever it is to finish you off, too.'

'Monkshood is a terrible poison,' I said as innocently as I was able.

Dr Briggs took a small bottle of iodine out of his bag and dabbed some onto a small square of lint. The sharp, medicinal tang filled the air as he cleaned my head.

'I don't know whether you've worked that out for yourself, or the police have told you.' He manoeuvred my head in all directions, checking his work in the overhead kitchen light. 'But yes, it's a deadly poison. Whatever Mr Miller may, or may not, have done, he didn't deserve that.'

'No one does,' I murmured.

Satisfied the wound was clean, and no deeper than it had looked when he first examined me outside, the doctor pressed a thick pad of gauze against it. With practised hands, he wound a long bandage round my head, tying the ends snugly above my ear so the dressing sat firm. 'That will keep it closed and stop the bleeding. I'm afraid you won't win any fashion contests, Mrs Miller, nor will you fit a hat over this bandage. Best to rest quietly this evening. If you feel giddy or sick, send for me at once.'

'Thank you, Doctor.'

'Now, am I to take you through to the parlour?' he asked. 'Or shall I tell the detective you are not well enough to be questioned?'

I smiled my thanks. 'I think I'd rather get it over with.'

'As you like.' He offered me his arm and I slowly got to my feet, swaying only slightly. 'One step at a time. If you feel dizzy, or faint, let me know immediately.'

I inclined my head, remembered it hurt to nod, and winced at the pounding that seemed to reverberate around my entire skull. 'I'll be all right.'

Dr Briggs pushed open the kitchen door and as we walked into the corridor, I could hear Detective Inspector Kennington questioning Maud and Ruby about what they had observed when they found me in the garden.

Luke, hearing our arrival, rushed to his feet and helped the doctor settle me in my favourite chair. For a moment, the room was quiet as everyone looked at me, the seriousness of what had happened perhaps hitting us all at the same time.

Detective Inspector Kennington broke the silence. 'I apologise, Mrs Miller, but I have some questions that won't wait until the morning. I'd like to start investigating the attack on you immediately and consider what it means for the case in general. One can't imagine that the two incidents are not linked.'

'Of course.' I smiled weakly at him.

The detective stared at Luke, who had remained at my side, his hand resting lightly on the back of my chair. 'Thank you, Vicar. That will be all.'

'We'll see you in the morning at church,' Ruby said brightly to fill the shocked silence at the detective's curt dismissal of Luke.

Maud sniffed. 'Detective or not, you should mind your manners. It's bad enough I'm sitting here in curlers without having to listen to you insult our vicar as well.'

'I think I've got all I need from you and Miss Andrews,' he said to Maud. 'Thank you for your time.'

If that was an attempt at an apology, it fell flat. Maud stopped to kiss my cheek before Ruby showed her to the front door. I could hear her muttering about how some people deserved a clip around the ear hole, and if she were not in her dressing gown, she'd be the one to do it.

Dr Briggs reminded me to rest before hurrying after Maud and Ruby. No doubt he wanted to hammer home his point about me not 'traipsing around the village' to the two women before he left.

'How can I help you?' I asked Detective Inspector

Kennington stiffly, half wishing I'd taken Dr Briggs up on his offer to tell the detective I wasn't well enough to speak to him.

'Someone clearly believes you pose a threat to them,' he said without preamble. 'That suggests either you've learned something significant about your husband's murder, or perhaps the killer wants you out of the way so they can control Mr Miller's finances. I understand he was a very wealthy man.'

'So I've been told.'

His pen hovered over his notebook. 'I need you to think carefully about every conversation you've had since this morning. What have you discovered that someone might kill to keep secret?'

The irony wasn't lost on me. Here was the same detective who had warned me off investigating only hours before I was attacked, now asking me to recount everything I'd learned through that very investigation. But I supposed attempted murder had a way of clarifying priorities.

'Well,' I began slowly, 'there's Bernard Harland's illegal pharmacy scheme. Lavinia Thompson told me she overheard Stan threatening to report Bernard if he didn't stop selling prescription medicines illegally.'

'Yes, Miss Thompson has somewhat belatedly spoken to us about this matter.' He made a note. 'What else?'

'Walter Preston's alleged involvement with Stan in questionable property deals. Stan was trying to make amends, but Preston refused to cooperate.' I touched my bandages gingerly. 'It may interest you to know that he has monkshood growing in his front garden and that he specifically asked his gardener to plant it there.'

'We're aware of Mr Preston's... activities. Anyone else?'

'I'm sure you already know that the village solicitor, Mr Beckwith, was stealing money meant for me. Stan confronted him about it the day before he died.'

Detective Inspector Kennington looked up from his writing. 'Mrs Miller, what strikes me about this list so far is that you seem to have made yourself known to every one of our suspects as someone actively investigating your husband's death.'

Heat rose in my cheeks, though whether from embarrassment or indignation, I wasn't certain. 'I've simply been having conversations with my neighbours and acquaintances. Naturally, the topic of Stan's death came up.'

'Naturally,' he repeated dryly. 'And in the course of these "conversations", you managed to uncover illegal pharmaceutical operations, property fraud, and embezzlement. Quite remarkable for casual village chatter.'

I said nothing, sensing that anything I might say would only dig me deeper into trouble.

He leaned forward slightly. 'Mrs Miller, I want to be very clear about something. This attack on you proves that we are dealing with someone who is prepared to use violence to protect themselves. Your amateur detecting has put you in serious danger.'

'But surely you can see that my investigation has been productive,' I protested. 'People tell me things they would never tell the police. In my opinion, I've uncovered motives you might never have found otherwise.'

'Perhaps. But you've also announced to the killer that you're closing in on them. Tonight's attack may have been intended as a warning – next time, they might not show such restraint.'

The thought sent a chill down my spine. I had been thinking of the attack as a sign that I was making progress, but Detective Inspector Kennington's interpretation was far more sobering.

'From this point forward,' he continued, 'I want you to cease all investigative activities. No more casual conversations, no more friendly visits to uncover information. Leave the detecting to the professionals.'

I wanted to argue, to point out that his professionals hadn't uncovered half of what I had learned. But the throbbing in my head reminded me of the very real danger I faced.

'I understand,' I said quietly.

He studied my face for a long moment, as if trying to determine whether I truly meant it. 'I hope you do, Mrs Miller. Because if you continue to interfere, you may not survive to see your husband's killer brought to justice. And that would be rather a shame, given it seems his death has left you a rather wealthy widow.'

The desire to protest – again – that I'd had nothing to do with Stan's death was strong. But the look the inspector gave Luke, hovering at my shoulder with obvious solicitous care, told me he'd already marked the vicar as a suspect. The last thing I wanted to do was say anything that would further raise the detective's suspicions towards Luke.

* * *

As soon as Luke and the detective left, Ruby came through with a mug of cocoa. 'If he'd lingered any longer, this would've been cold – and I'm certain that simply doesn't do anyone any good.'

'Thank you.' I wrapped my hands around the mug. I blinked away the tears that gathered in my eyes. 'How did you know this is exactly what I needed?'

She smiled. 'Because it's exactly what I needed myself. Goodness, Martha, when I saw you on the grass and realised you were bleeding... well, it was terrifying.'

'I'm glad you and Maud heard Lizzy and came to help me.'

'I think she probably scared the attacker off,' Ruby said. 'As soon as she started barking, I put on my bedside light and peered out of the window.'

'She deserves a special treat.' I reached down and patted Lizzy's head. 'Maybe Farmer Bennington has something he can send our way for her. If not, I'll do without meat for the week so Lizzy can have my share.'

'Ben thinks we should postpone the wedding.'

'What?' I cried. 'No! Whatever for?'

'He thinks it might be in bad taste for us to celebrate a wedding only a week after Stan's death. Probably only a few days after he's laid to rest.' Ruby gave a small shrug as though it didn't matter, but I could tell she was trying to be brave. 'Also, if Stan's killer, and the person who attacked you, haven't been caught then he'll be very busy working.'

'I was going to say I thought I wasn't cut out for investigating any more,' I admitted. 'But this news makes me even more determined that I should continue.'

'I'd rather you didn't if it means you will get bashed on the head again,' Ruby said. 'Or worse.'

'But you don't want to delay the wedding, do you?'

'Oh Martha, of course not.' She bit her lip as though she was going to say something else, but then thought better of it.

I thought back to Maud's remark earlier that morning, and the one made by Dr Briggs when we were outside. I waited a beat, but Ruby didn't say anything more.

'Then I shall jolly well carry on until I know who the killer is.'

'What about your safety?'

'I shall ensure I never go anywhere alone,' I said. 'Perhaps I'll suggest Maud brings a rolling pin in that cavernous handbag of hers.'

'You shouldn't make jokes,' Ruby admonished. 'You could have been very badly injured tonight.'

'Who said I'm joking?' I retorted, and touched my head. 'This bandage will keep my head safe, and I can just see Maud brandishing her rolling pin at anyone who gets too close.'

Despite my show of bravery in front of Ruby, I was worried about my ability to find the killer. Perhaps I had just been lucky on the previous occasions I had found killers before the police. After all, I was just a village housewife, not a detective. What business did I have questioning suspects and examining evidence? What if my amateur meddling was putting other people, and not just myself, in danger?

'Ben is right. Detective Inspector Kennington is right. Doctor Briggs is certainly right. You should stay home, and not carry on. It isn't safe.'

'Neither is taking Lizzy out for a late-night visit to the garden,' I quipped. 'The person who attacked me tonight knows I'm investigating. They're frightened enough of what I might discover to try to stop me. The detective asked me to repeat what I've found out, but how am I supposed to know which conversation I had, and with whom, was the one that made the killer panic?'

'Well, we know it wasn't Luke.'

'Yes, we do. That's the only thing I am certain of.'

'Aren't you certain he didn't kill Stan?'

'I wish I was,' I admitted. 'Though it makes little sense that he killed Stan and then I was coincidentally attacked by someone who is not at all linked to Stan's death.'

'I hate to give Maud-like advice.' Ruby grimaced. 'But you should probably sleep on it. Perhaps the answer will be clearer in the morning.'

'Tomorrow is Sunday,' I said. 'No one can complain if I go to church and just happen to speak with friends, can they?'

Ruby raised an eyebrow. 'Since when have Walter Preston and Oliver Beckwith been friends?'

'Neighbours, then,' I corrected, then lightly patted my head. 'Imagine how many people will want to talk to me when they see my bandage. The whole village will want to know exactly what happened, and who knows what they may have seen.'

'You're ingenious, aren't you?'

I gave a modest little shrug. 'Maud says I have a devious mind.'

'Whichever – ingenious or devious – I'm very proud of the way you solve crimes.' Ruby took my empty mug from my hands. 'Come along, Martha. If you want to be at church early for as much tea and sympathy as you can handle, we had better get to bed.'

We hugged on the landing, then went our separate ways. Of course I wanted Stan's murder solved before the wedding. But after that, Ruby would be gone, and I had grown used to her laughter, her company – used to not being alone.

10

The air that Sunday was crisp, as was usual for an English spring morning. Ruby was accompanying me to church because I was hoping to speak to Luke before the service began. No one would question the two of us talking to the vicar – after all, we could be discussing arrangements for Ruby's wedding the following week.

However, if I was to be seen talking to Luke alone, tongues would wag. Certainly people would already be talking about me and the sudden death of my husband so soon after his return to Westleham, but I didn't want them to be gossiping about Luke.

'Are you sure you should be coming to church this morning?' Ruby eyed me dubiously. 'Your colour is still very pale.'

I shrugged. 'I'm always pale, Ruby. It comes with having fair hair and freckled skin.'

My colouring was what I thought people optimistically called 'English rose', which really meant pale with a tendency to burn. Ruby, on the other hand, was rather glamorous with her dyed blonde hair, red lips, and a pretty bloom in her cheeks that had nothing to do with cosmetics.

'You know what I mean,' she said quietly. 'After last night, I'm worried about you.'

She had linked her arm through mine. I reached over and squeezed her hand. 'I know you are, but I promise I won't leave your sight for the entire service.'

Ruby grinned then. 'That bandage is extremely dramatic.'

I smiled back. 'I think Dr Briggs made it as big and ugly as he could. He probably thought it would make me stay home. However, it works in my favour too. I think people will want to talk to me about what happened. The more they discuss it, the more likely someone is to let slip something useful.'

The churchyard was quiet, as it should be a full half an hour before the morning service. Most villagers would be finishing breakfast and preparing for their weekly ritual of community worship and gossip.

We made our way around to the vestry and I knocked lightly on the door. If Luke was surprised to see us so early, it didn't show on his face.

'Mrs Miller, Miss Andrews,' he said in an overly loud voice. 'I assume you are here to discuss the arrangements for the flowers next week?'

'Yes,' Ruby said, matching the pitch of Luke's voice. 'Though I did want to make you aware that Ben is rather worried about the family having a wedding so closely after my brother-in-law's untimely death.'

'Of course,' Luke said, then stood back. 'Well, come inside, ladies, and we will discuss all eventualities.'

He closed the door leading to the main church and sat at the small desk. 'How are you feeling, Martha?'

'Better than I look,' I assured him.

'I'm certain Doctor Briggs advised you to rest.' He glanced at Ruby. 'I'm also worried about your safety.'

'I'm quite safe here,' I said. 'And I needed to ask you some questions.'

Luke sighed. 'I rather thought you might.'

'What did Frank tell you about the monkshood in the churchyard?'

'He told me Preston wanted to have some in his front garden.' Luke shook his head in disbelief. 'Apparently the fellow thought the purple flowers of the monkshood would look good next to his pink geraniums.'

'Did you know how poisonous it is?'

'I knew monkshood was poisonous,' he said. 'But I hadn't been aware until asked if he could dig some up just how dangerous it is. Neither had I known the plant grew so prolifically in the churchyard.'

'You didn't know what it looked like?'

'I didn't,' he confirmed. 'As I've said, I knew the plant was dangerous. It's one of those things one hears about in the country, but I wasn't aware it was in the churchyard. As soon as I knew, and Frank pointed it out, I told him he could dig as much of it up as he liked.'

'When was this?'

'Earlier in the week.'

'Before Stan came back?'

'Yes,' Luke said. 'Which, I suppose, keeps me firmly on the suspect list.'

'Do the police know?'

'I've been open and honest with them.' He looked so intently at me, I was sure he could see me thinking through the conversation we had the afternoon before Stan died. 'Just as I have with you. As I always have with you.'

'I am glad the police know. It will help them to believe you didn't harm Stan.'

'What about you?' he asked, his blue eyes dark with hurt. 'You need to ask me the question, don't you?'

I didn't pretend to misunderstand him. I thought I knew the truth, but he was right, I did need to ask. 'Did you kill Stan?'

Ruby gasped, clearly shocked that I had voiced my worst fears.

'No, I did not.' His voice was calm and firm. 'I understand that you're investigating Stan's murder and so you have to question everyone – even those closest to you. But I can't pretend I'm not upset that you needed to ask me.'

'I'm sorry.' The words felt inadequate when his pain was so obvious. 'But please know, I don't doubt you.'

'You're being thorough,' he said with so much understanding, it made me feel worse to have asked him that question. 'I know what it is I said that made you scared I was involved. I meant what I said. But I would never, could never, do something that would bring about someone else's demise. Even if that person was a barrier to my own happiness.'

His words made me feel ashamed I'd needed to ask him to confirm his innocence. Voices came from the main part of the church, and it reminded me that life was going on in Westleham. People were going about their day – including the person who had killed Stan.

'I need to keep investigating.'

'You haven't asked me about last night.'

'Last night?' I frowned.

'When you were attacked.'

'Why would I need to ask you about that?'

'Surely whoever killed Stan then attacked you last night in an attempt to stop you looking into his death? For it to be unconnected would be rather a coincidence.'

'I agree.' I reached out and rested a hand on his arm for a

moment, needing to feel a connection between us, no matter how small. 'I didn't need to ask you about that because I never thought, even for a second, that you were the one who attacked me.'

The sound of the church door opening and closing echoed through the building. Luke glanced at me and sighed. 'People are beginning to arrive. Martha, please—'

'I'll be careful,' I promised, knowing what he was about to say.

He nodded, gave Ruby a quick smile, then opened the door leading to the church. 'Glad we have that issue resolved. Let me know if you, or Ben, have any further thoughts about postponing your wedding.'

We stepped out of the vestry onto the path alongside the church and walked around to the main entrance. 'I can't believe you asked the poor man if he killed Stan!'

'I had to,' I said miserably.

'It would serve you right if he was so upset with you that he completely falls out of love with you.'

'He's not—'

'Oh, Martha, do stop.' Ruby shook her head. 'You can't pretend with me.'

'You can't pretend with me,' I retorted before I could stop myself.

She flushed. 'What do you mean?'

'Does Ben know the real reason why you're so keen for the wedding not to be postponed?'

'He does not,' she said stiffly. 'And I'm not going to tell him.'

'I'd better hurry up and uncover the murderer then, hadn't I?'

'Yes, you had,' Ruby said with gusto. 'I wouldn't want the village busybodies counting on their fingers and realising things happened a little out of sequence. Ben would be dreadfully embarrassed.'

'Let's get into church and allow the gossiping about my attack begin.' I linked arms with my sister, then leaned close as I whispered, 'I'm awfully excited about becoming an auntie.'

Saying the words out loud made them real. I was excited. Perhaps even six months ago, I would've been horribly jealous. But not any more. Ruby and I were so close these days, her happiness was at least as important to me as my own.

Ruby blinked away the tears that formed in her eyes. 'I understand my part: I must talk about how Lizzy barking woke me up and see if anyone tells me they saw someone out late last night. We're going to solve this, Martha, and I'm going to have my wedding!'

'I'm sure you're right and between the two of us, and Maud, we'll have a wealth of new knowledge by lunchtime.'

I adjusted my bandage one final time and prepared to discover just how much sympathy – and information – a wounded woman could extract from her concerned neighbours.

* * *

Luke's sermon was unlike anything I had ever heard from him before. He was never a fire-and-brimstone preacher. His usual tone was kindness, understanding, and a heavy measure of God's mercy. Today, however, he seemed to be speaking straight to the killer's conscience.

Eyes sweeping the congregation, he paused, then said in a voice that rang through the church: 'Heed the warning given so clearly by Moses in Numbers: "But if ye will not do so, behold, ye have sinned against the Lord: and be sure your sin will find you out."'

I half expected the guilty person to run from the church, unable to sit still given the relentless conviction in Luke's words and delivery.

Unfortunately, no one wanted to make my mission to find the killer easier and out themselves. No matter; as always, I would rely on my sleuthing skills to uncover Stan's murderer.

Bernard Harland sat with his brother Ted three rows in front of us. His dark head was bent attentively towards Luke, as though he were hanging on Luke's every word. Ted, on the other hand, fidgeted and looked uncomfortable.

Walter Preston occupied his usual place near the front, his wife beside him, posture rigid, as though a ruler had been pressed against her back. I couldn't see Oliver Beckwith though I was certain he would be in attendance, and would probably try to garner sympathy for his injury. Though, of course, for very different reasons than me.

Annie and Lavinia were sitting in a pew across the aisle from me. They both had their hands folded in their laps, expressions neutral, as they listened to Luke.

As the final hymn ended and the congregation began to file out, I prepared myself for the onslaught of concerned neighbours. Ruby squeezed my arm encouragingly.

'I'll move between the conversations,' she whispered, 'and listen for anyone who mentions if they saw someone out late last night.'

The moment we stepped into the foyer of the church, we were surrounded. It seemed every person in Westleham wanted to express their shock at the attack and examine my dramatic bandaging.

'Oh, my goodness, Martha!' Ada Bennington hurried over, her face creased with worry. 'When I heard what happened, I could barely believe it. Who would do such a thing?'

'I wish I knew,' I replied, touching my bandage gingerly. 'It's rather frightening to think someone was lurking in my garden.'

'You poor dear,' cooed Mrs Taylor, the owner of the village haberdashery shop. 'You must have been terrified. Did you get a good look at whoever it was?'

I shook my head carefully, mindful of moving too quickly in any direction. 'It was too dark, and everything happened so quickly. One moment I was watching Lizzy sniff about the garden, the next I was waking up on the ground with Ruby and Mrs Burnett looking scared to death.'

A small crowd had gathered around us, and I noticed Maud positioning herself strategically near a different group of villagers. She caught my eye and nodded almost imperceptibly – she was busy listening to village gossip.

'Dreadful business,' said Joe Noble, who ran the Cricketer's Arms with his wife, Winnie. 'First poor Stan, now this attack on you. Makes a person wonder if Westleham is safe any more.'

'Were you serving at the pub late last night, Mr Noble?' I asked, as though making casual conversation. 'I'm trying to narrow down who the attacker could be.'

'I closed up at the usual time,' he replied. 'The bar was quite busy, as it usually is on a Saturday. Though I did see that fellow from Brighton – Bernard Harland – coming back to his room as I was locking up. He was on his own, which struck me as odd since he and his brother have seemed inseparable since they arrived.'

Bernard walking alone at that hour was certainly interesting, especially given what Lavinia had overheard the night before Stan died, and that I had been attacked around the time the pub would be closing.

'Perhaps he couldn't sleep,' suggested Mrs Taylor. 'Some people find a walk helps settle their nerves.'

'Or perhaps he had business to attend to,' said a sharp voice behind me. I turned to see Winnie Noble approaching with her usual disapproving expression. She looked pointedly at my bandage. 'I do hope, Mrs Miller, that this terrible incident won't prevent you from making proper arrangements for your husband's funeral. One would have thought that would be foremost in your mind, not your sister's wedding. Especially given you have been left in such an advantageous position.'

The implication was crystal clear, and heat rose in my cheeks. 'I beg your pardon, Mrs Noble?'

'Don't play the innocent with me,' she replied. 'The whole village knows Mr Miller has left you very well off. How fortunate for you.'

I wasn't sure how anyone could possibly know Stan had accumulated substantial wealth before his death, or that I had been discussing Ruby's wedding, and not Stan's funeral, that morning, but it shouldn't surprise me. Nothing stayed secret in Westleham for long.

'One day listening at the doors of your paying guests will get you into trouble,' Maud said sweetly. 'Imagine if the village came to believe their every whisper was fodder for your gossip – you'd have no guests left to pour your precious afternoon tea for.'

'Well really!' Winnie flounced off, the amused laughs of several villagers following her.

'Mrs Miller?' Iris caught hold of my arm. 'Might I have a word?'

'Of course.' I walked to the side of the church, away from listening ears. 'What is it, Iris?'

'Last night, very late last night, I saw Oliver Beckwith's office lights on. I don't know if it's important, but I thought you should know.'

'Should I ask why you were out late last night, Iris?'

She looked down at the floor. 'No, Mrs Miller, you should not.'

'I see,' I said gently. 'I don't know if you heard what Mrs Noble just said to me, but you surely know what village gossip is like by now. It's only a matter of time before you and Frank are caught out. Please don't let it come to that.'

'I'll talk to Frank.' Iris bit her lip. 'But you won't say where you heard the information about Oliver Beckwith from?'

'I won't,' I confirmed.

Frank Bennington joined us then. He and Iris shared such a sweet smile that anyone who was looking in their direction would have no doubt as to the nature of their relationship.

'I was sorry to hear what happened to you,' he said. 'I assume Iris has told you about Oliver Beckwith's office lights?'

'She has.' I gave a small nod.

'When I was on my way home, I saw Walter Preston standing in his front garden smoking a cigar.' He shrugged. 'It might not mean anything – he could have just been smoking outside because his wife doesn't like the smell or something – but I thought it best to let you know.'

'That's very helpful, Frank, thank you.'

'Mrs Miller thinks we should talk to Luke,' Iris said. 'Before he finds out from someone else.'

Frank looked doubtfully over to where Luke was talking with parishioners as they left the church. 'I'm not sure.'

'Perhaps you're not as keen on me as you say.'

I couldn't help but admire Iris's change in demeanour. Her eyes were downcast, and she shuffled her feet and looked as though she might be on the verge of tears.

'Oh I am, Iris, I am!' he declared. 'Look, if it means that much to you, I shall go ask your brother if we can walk out together.'

'Now?' she asked.

'Yes,' he replied boldly. 'Right now.'

Frank marched off and Iris smiled at me. 'Goodness. That was a little easier than I thought it would be.'

'I'm no expert on relationships, but I think that means Frank is very fond of you.'

'I should go and see what Luke says.' Iris walked away a few steps, then turned back. 'I hope you find out who killed your husband very soon, Mrs Miller.'

'Let's get you home.' Ruby appeared at my side and linked an arm through mine. 'You're looking a little peaky.'

I didn't protest because it was true that I wasn't feeling my best. Although the hammering in my head had subsided to a dull ache, I still felt weak and a little trembly as though standing up for long periods of time was exhausting.

When we returned home, I thought it might help to get out a piece of paper and make notes about everything we knew so far. That would help me work out what questions I needed to ask next.

The investigation was gaining speed and I wanted to be at the front of the race to find Stan's killer.

* * *

As we reached the gate between the churchyard and the path, I heard someone calling my name.

'Mrs Miller? Might I have a word?'

I turned to see Ted Harland approaching, his usually warm face etched with worry. He glanced nervously over his shoulder before joining us.

'Of course, Mr Harland,' I replied. 'Why don't you follow my sister and me to our home? We can talk there without being overheard by half of the village.'

He nodded and then hurried out of the gate and across the road, as though worried someone would see him coming home with us.

Ted refused my offer of refreshments and looked at me in concern as he sat opposite me at the kitchen table.

'I... I hardly know where to begin,' he said, wringing his hands. 'This whole business has me completely at sixes and sevens. First Stan, now this attack on you...'

'It's been a difficult time for all of us,' I said gently. 'It was easy to see that you and Stan were very close friends.'

His eyes filled with tears, and for a moment I thought he might break down entirely. 'We were, which is why I can't help feeling so responsible. If I hadn't convinced Stan to come back to Westleham, he'd still be alive.'

'You mustn't blame yourself,' Ruby interjected kindly. 'From what I understand, Stan made his own decision to return and make amends. That speaks well of his character.'

'Yes, but...' Ted looked down at the table. 'There are things you don't know. Things about why Stan really felt he had to come back.'

My pulse quickened. 'What do you mean – in addition to his dealings with Walter Preston?'

He nodded. 'In Brighton, Stan had been doing well with his investments, as I told you. But he'd also been... well, he'd been helping certain people with their financial difficulties. People who'd lost money through unfortunate circumstances.'

'What kind of circumstances?' I asked carefully.

Ted's face reddened with embarrassment. 'Gambling, Mrs Miller, and I'm afraid my brother Bernard was one of the people he was helping. I didn't know at first, but it turns out Bernard had accumulated some rather significant gambling debts. Stan had been helping him manage them, but recently the situation had become quite desperate.'

I tried not to react too much to Ted's words, but I knew from experience that desperate people did desperate things. 'How desperate?'

'Enough that Bernard had started taking shortcuts in his business practices.' Ted's voice dropped to barely above a whisper. 'I'm embarrassed to admit it, but Bernard was selling prescription medication to people.'

'Goodness,' I murmured, shocked that Ted knew about the scheme. Why had Stan told Bernard that if he didn't stop, he would tell Ted all about it? 'How terrible.'

'Stan discovered what Bernard was doing about a month ago. He was furious – not just about the illegal activity, but about the fact that Bernard was using the money Stan had lent him to cover his gambling losses.'

'Stan told you?'

Ted smiled sadly. 'Stan and I didn't have secrets. He told me as soon as he found out what Bernard was doing.'

'Did you talk to your brother about what he was doing?'

'I didn't,' he said. 'Stan thought it was best he handled it. He believed that if he warned Bernard he'd tell me what was going on unless Bernard changed his ways, the fear of being exposed would be enough to shame him into giving it up.'

'So Stan threatened to reveal the truth to you unless he stopped?'

'More than that.' Ted shook his head, his expression fearful. 'When it was clear the threat to tell me wasn't enough, Stan told Bernard he would report him to the authorities if Bernard didn't cease his actions immediately.'

'Your brother must have been furious.'

'Indeed. Stan said they had terrible rows about it. That was one of the reasons he wanted to come back here and set his own affairs straight – he said he couldn't demand honesty from others if he hadn't been honest himself.'

The picture was becoming clearer, and more troubling. 'Mr Harland, do you know where your brother was last night?'

Ted's face went very pale. 'We were downstairs in the pub for some time, and I went up to bed at about ten. Bernard said he was staying in the bar until closing time. However, I found it hard to sleep, so thought I would go to the bathroom to get a drink of water.'

'Go on,' I said breathlessly.

'As I was going into the bathroom, I heard a noise and turned around. That's when I saw Bernard coming up the stairs and going towards his room.'

'Did he see you?'

'I know he didn't.' Ted shook his head. 'When I confronted Bernard this morning about where he'd been last night, he said I was wrong and that I must have seen him when he was going to the bathroom. That can't be true, Mrs Miller, because I was outside the bathroom, and Bernard was coming up the stairs!'

'Where do you think he'd been?'

'I don't know,' he said miserably, and gestured at my bandaged head. 'When I found out you had been attacked, I couldn't help but wonder if Bernard was involved. It's positively dreadful. Stan's murder, and now what happened to you – I'm starting to fear what Bernard might be capable of.'

The implications were staggering. Not only did this mean Bernard had no alibi for the time of my attack, but neither did Ted.

'Mr Harland, I'm very sorry to hear about your brother's activities,' I said carefully, 'but I also need to ask you directly: where were you last night between eleven and midnight?'

He looked startled by the question, then understanding dawned on his face. 'Oh. Oh dear. I see what you mean. I was in my room at the pub, Mrs Miller. I can't prove it, of course, since no one can vouch for me, but I can tell you truthfully that I was nowhere near your garden last night.'

I studied his face, trying to read his sincerity. Ted Harland seemed genuinely distressed and frightened, quite different from his brother's calculated composure. But appearances could be deceiving, particularly when it came to murder.

'One more question,' I said. 'Do you know if Bernard has knowledge of poisons or poisonous plants?'

Ted nodded reluctantly. 'His pharmaceutical training included toxicology, naturally. But more than that – during the war, he served with a medical unit that dealt with gas attacks and other chemical injuries. He knows far more about poisons and their effects than most people ever would.'

Ted left soon afterwards, looking more dejected than he had the previous day when Stan died. Out of the two brothers, Bernard remained the most obvious suspect, but I couldn't rule out Ted entirely. Despite his brother's illegal activities, Ted was clearly very fond of him.

It was possible Ted had killed Stan to prevent him from reporting Bernard's fraud to the authorities. Surely he had more loyalty to his brother than to a friend, however close Stan and Ted had been.

But would a man so loyal to his brother that he would commit murder to keep his secrets then implicate that brother in a murder? Because that is what Ted Harland had just done.

He had painted an increasingly desperate picture of Bernard – a man with mounting debts and facing exposure of his illegal activities. Such a person might well resort to murder to protect himself.

11

No sooner had Ted Harland left than the familiar squeak of the gate between my garden and Maud's heralded my neighbour's imminent arrival.

I fetched a pen and paper in readiness for the notes I wanted to make on what we had learned so far, and to determine the gaps in our knowledge. Writing everything down helped me see patterns I might otherwise have missed.

'Where shall we start?' Maud asked as she opened her knitting bag and pulled out a pink, almost finished, matinee jacket.

'Let's go through each suspect and what we know about them. Specifically, we need to work through whether they could have killed Stan. Then where they were, so far as we are aware, for the attack on me. Hopefully that will narrow down further questions I need to ask, as well as anyone that we feel that we can eliminate.'

'I wonder if Detective Inspector Kennington is doing the same thing,' Ruby mused. 'I didn't see him in church this morning.'

'Of course your beau was there.' Maud gave Ruby a wink.

'He certainly was,' Ruby said. 'We don't want to start our married life off skipping church. How would it look if we want the vicar to marry us next week but we couldn't be bothered to turn up this morning?'

I only hoped Ben wouldn't insist on delaying the wedding because, as Ruby had admitted to me earlier, they had rather jumped the gun in respect to certain domestic arrangements. After Stan's desertion, reappearance, and murder, our family had been the subject of more than its fair share of village gossip. I desperately didn't want that for Ruby.

'I should hope he is,' I said. 'Any detective worth his salt should be spending today gathering their thoughts and preparing for the final push to uncover the murderer.'

'While I remember,' Ruby said, 'I invited Ben over for dinner. Is that all right?'

'Of course.' I smiled, hoping I would continue to see them both for Sunday dinner every week but knowing that they might want to start their own family traditions. 'We had better get on with things. If I'm to investigate, get dinner on, and get home before Ben gets here then I don't have a lot of time.'

'Yes, you'll be in trouble if he finds you've been out sleuthing instead of resting as his colleague advised,' Maud teased.

'Ben knows Martha well enough by now to know that she isn't very good at heeding advice when it aims to prevent her from investigating.'

'Right then,' I said, spreading my papers across the table. 'Let's see where we are.'

Maud peered at my handwriting over her spectacles. 'Your penmanship has deteriorated since that bang to your head.'

'Never mind the quality of my writing. Look at the facts.' I pointed to the list I'd compiled. 'Let's start with the current most likely suspect: Bernard Harland. He has the pharmaceutical knowledge, and we already know it's not hard to find monkshood in the village, though it's also possible he planned Stan's murder and brought the poison with him. He had a motive – Stan was threatening to expose his illegal prescription scheme. And according to his own brother, he was not at the Cricketer's Arms at the time I was attacked.'

'And we know he had the opportunity for Stan's murder,' Maud said. 'He could have easily put monkshood into Stan's gloves at any point before Stan went in to bat because the gloves were in the pavilion all morning.'

Maud nodded slowly. 'Who next? Walter Preston with monkshood in his garden?'

'Also another likely suspect. If Stan reported Preston's property deals it would ruin him. If not financially, certainly socially. He would be ostracised in the village and while I don't think he would care very much, his wife would not be able to stand it.'

'Could it be proven after all this time?' Ruby wondered.

'If Stan made a statement giving details of his involvement, then possibly. However, without Stan, there's no case against Walter Preston. Unless there's a written record of what Stan did, I think the case dies with him. Which of course is the main reason I think that Mr Preston should remain towards the top of my list.'

'What about the attack on you?'

'Frank Bennington saw him late last night when he was on his way home. He said Mr Preston was in his front garden smoking a cigar.'

Ruby frowned. 'How does that matter?'

'It shows that he was not only awake, but fully dressed, at approximately half past eleven. He could easily have just returned from hitting me, or was just about to go and do it.'

'I suppose Frank was too distracted to know the exact time he was walking home?' Maud asked with a raised eyebrow.

'It seems so,' I said. 'Though after I spoke to him and Iris this morning, he did go and speak to Luke. Hopefully he will stop sneaking around the village with Iris and call at the vicarage properly to take her out.'

'Thank goodness,' Ruby breathed. 'I'm not very good at keeping secrets.'

Maud eyed Ruby with a mischievous gleam in her eye. 'I don't know, dear. I think you're much better at it than you think.'

'Moving along,' I said quickly. 'Iris also told me that as Frank took her home, they couldn't help but notice that Oliver Beckwith's lights were on in his office. Of course, that doesn't mean it was Mr Beckwith in there, but I can't imagine anyone else has keys to his offices.'

'We know he had good reason to want Stan out of the way,' Ruby said, with a clear effort not to use either 'murder' or 'killed'. 'But as I understand it, the police are looking into his business dealings generally so perhaps his motive wouldn't be as strong. He's in trouble with the law anyway, isn't he?'

'I believe so,' I said. 'And even though he gave me a cheque for the amount of money Stan left for me, he didn't do it until he was caught out.'

Maud frowned. 'He also needs to be at the top of the list. Who else do you have, Martha?'

'Ted Harland told me he saw his brother coming back to the Cricketer's Arms late last night. However, his brother did not see him, so Ted does not have an alibi for the attack on me.'

'Do you really think he might have killed Stan?' Ruby asked. 'They seemed such good chums.'

'I think Ted is more loyal to his brother than to Stan,' I said carefully. 'He admitted Stan was intending to report Bernard to the authorities if he didn't stop his illegal activities. It's possible Ted wanted to protect his brother and so decided to silence Stan.'

'I agree with Ruby.' Maud looked up, but her needles did not stop their rhythmic clackety-clack. 'He needs to be further down the list.'

'Is there anyone else?'

'Yes, Ruby, I don't think we can discount Lavinia Thompson.'

'Really?'

'Oh yes,' I said. 'You didn't see her face when Stan denied that their relationship had been serious. She was both devastated and furious in equal measures.'

'But surely she wouldn't have hit you with a tree branch?' Ruby asked doubtfully.

'If she was angry enough at Stan to kill him, it stands to reason she was also resentful enough of me, the woman Stan chose to be his wife, to also want me dead.'

'I suppose that's true.' Maud stopped knitting and pointed at my list. 'Put her at the bottom of the list.'

I raised an eyebrow. 'Below Luke?'

'Of course not,' she snapped. 'Don't be ridiculous. No one is less likely to bash you over the head in your own garden than Luke.'

'Do we agree that Luke is no longer a suspect?'

'I imagine he will be towards the top of the police's list,' Ruby said. 'But for our purposes, the attack on you removes him from suspicion in Stan's death. I agree with Maud. He adores you, Martha. He would rather leave Westleham and never see you again than hurt you.'

'He hasn't said such a thing, has he?' I asked quickly, panic edging my voice.

'Well—' Ruby looked horribly uncomfortable.

'Ruby?'

'He did say something like that when we met for him to bless the cottage. But, of course, that was when he thought Stan might be coming back to Westleham.'

Such a thing had never crossed my mind. It was the sort of honourable thing Luke would say, but I hated that he had ever had such a thought. No matter the circumstances either of us were in, I couldn't imagine never seeing Luke again.

* * *

An hour later, Maud and I were walking through the village, planning to call on Lavinia Thompson at the Cricketer's Arms. I wanted to see if I could carefully ask where she had been the previous evening, and if she had remembered anything more about the argument she'd overheard between Stan and Bernard.

After calling at the pub, we were shown up to Annie Raynor's room, where we were told the two women were waiting for their lunch. The smell of food cooking permeated the building and made my stomach rumble. I could only hope the dinner Ruby had insisted she cook would smell half as good. However, Ruby, even by her own admission, had trouble boiling water, let alone cooking a full meal.

'Mrs Miller,' Annie said with a smile. 'How are you feeling? That bandage looks very dramatic.'

'It does, doesn't it. But Dr Briggs is an excellent doctor; he assures me the large bandage is necessary,' I replied, settling carefully into a chair. 'I'm much better, thank you. I was hoping to ask Lavinia a few more questions about what she overheard the other night.'

Lavinia set down her sewing and looked at me attentively. 'Of course. How can I help, Mrs Miller?'

'I'm wondering if you remembered anything else about the

conversation between Stan and Bernard Harland? I often find that details come back to witnesses later.'

Lavinia frowned in concentration. 'I've been thinking about it quite a lot, actually. There was one thing – Bernard said something about "the arrangement" and how Stan had no right to interfere with it. Stan replied that any arrangement built on dishonesty was bound to fail.'

'Did he say what the arrangement was?' Maud asked, leaning forward slightly.

'Not specifically, but from the context, I gathered it was the prescription scheme. Stan said something about consequences and how Bernard needed to think about what he was doing to people who trusted him. Then Bernard laughed – it was a rather unpleasant sound, actually – and said that Stan was hardly one to lecture about trust, given what he'd done with the information he had learned from his job at the bank which he then passed on.'

This was interesting. Lavinia had not said she knew about Stan's dealings with Walter Preston when we had spoken to her the previous day. Given her fondness for Stan, perhaps that wasn't surprising.

'Did Stan respond to that?'

'Yes, he sounded very upset but repeated his plea for Bernard to stop his scheming. That was when Bernard said he hoped Stan was ready for the consequences of his interference.'

'I see.' Lavinia had remembered a little more than she had yesterday. That wasn't unusual; people often remembered more when they'd had a little time to think about things. However, it seemed rather a big thing for her to recall twenty-four hours after her original statement to me. 'Miss Thompson, where were you last night? I apologise for the slightly accusatory tone of the question, but I'm asking everyone the same thing. I'm trying to narrow down who might have attacked me, you understand.'

'Oh, Mrs Miller,' Annie said. 'Isn't that rather dangerous? What if you ask the murderer and they come back and finish what they started last night?'

'I rather hope I do ask the murderer,' I retorted. 'Otherwise I'm not doing a very good job at sleuthing if Stan's killer isn't on my list of suspects.'

'Am I a suspect?' Lavinia's face flushed a deep crimson.

'Everyone who had a disagreement with, or who was upset with Stan, has to be a suspect. I hope you understand that, Miss Thompson.'

Something seemed to occur to Annie and she turned to look at her friend. 'Where were you, Miss Thompson? For I know that you were not in your room.'

'Of course I was.'

'I knocked on your door to return the scissors you had kindly lent me earlier in the evening,' Annie said. 'There was no answer.'

'What time was that?' I asked.

'Oh, it was rather late,' Annie replied. 'After eleven. Ordinarily I wouldn't dream of calling so late, but Miss Thompson has told me several times in the past that she often has trouble sleeping.'

'I expect I was asleep.'

'You were not,' Annie said quietly. 'When there was no answer, I thought to just put the scissors on the table, so you had them in case you needed them. You must have gone on one of your late-night walks again.'

'Oh, silly me.' Lavinia smiled brightly. 'You're right, I did go for a walk. I was so upset over Stan's horrible death that I actually went and sat in the church for a time where I prayed that his killer would be found quickly.'

'I see.'

'I'm so sorry, Mrs Miller.' Lavinia's gaze dropped to her hands, which were folded neatly in her lap. 'As I told you yesterday, I was embarrassed my feelings for Mr Miller were not returned. I was rather hurt by his cruel dismissal of me. I told you I was cross with him, and so did not tell the police about Mr Harland threatening him. I'm sure you can understand that after his death I felt so very guilty about that.'

'So you went to pray for forgiveness.' Annie sounded very relieved her friend had a reasonable excuse for not being in her room. 'I'm sure you have nothing to feel guilty about, dear, but I can certainly see why you would seek solace in the church.'

Her story wasn't unreasonable – I knew that Luke never locked the church. However, it did mean that she was not in her room when I was attacked. I was surprised. Out of all the suspects, I thought Miss Thompson was most likely to be tucked up in bed for the night, not walking about the village.

'Of course, yes,' I said in a tone that I hoped was reassuring. 'That makes perfect sense.'

'Why did you say that?' Maud asked as we walked down the stairs from Annie's room. We hadn't stayed long after Lavinia's revelation – partly because I couldn't think of a single thing more to ask, but mostly because I wanted to get home and see how Ruby was getting along with dinner. 'It doesn't make perfect sense at all.'

'It's possible.'

'Possible? What rot,' Maud scoffed. 'Who goes and sits in a cold village church in the middle of the night, regardless of how guilty they may feel?'

'Do you think she did it, then?' I asked. 'Killed Stan, and bludgeoned me over the head?'

'Ah, now I didn't say that.' Maud backtracked faster than a mouse who'd spotted a cat. 'I'm simply saying her church story is nonsense.'

'We still have five viable suspects.' I sighed. 'I had hoped to be down to four after speaking to Miss Thompson.'

'I suppose you'll be wanting to speak to Bernard Harland while we're here?'

'Yes, then we should go and check on Ruby. I don't want her to burn dinner and have Ben think she's a terrible cook.'

'She is a terrible cook.'

'Well, yes.' I smiled at Maud – one could always rely on her to tell the absolute truth. 'But we don't want Ben knowing that.'

'I shouldn't think it'll matter at this stage,' Maud said wisely. 'He's committed to marrying her and, as he's a detective, I rather think he will have worked out the reason you always cook the meals in your house.'

As usual, I was certain Maud's assessment of the situation was accurate.

* * *

Bernard Harland was sitting alone in the public bar of the Cricketer's Arms, nursing what looked like a whisky, despite it being barely past lunchtime. The room was otherwise empty, most of the village having returned home after church to prepare their Sunday dinners.

'Mr Harland,' I said, approaching his table with Maud at my side. 'Might we join you for a moment?'

He looked up, and I was struck by how exhausted he appeared. Dark circles shadowed his eyes, and his usually immaculate appearance was somewhat dishevelled – his collar slightly askew, his hair not quite as carefully arranged as it had been at church.

'Mrs Miller. Mrs Burnett.' He gestured to the empty chairs. 'Please, sit down. I imagine you have more questions for me. I saw my brother approach you after the service ended.'

His directness caught me off guard. I'd been prepared to ease into the conversation, to employ the subtle approach that had served me well with other suspects. But Bernard's weary forthrightness seemed to render such tactics unnecessary.

'I do have questions, yes,' I admitted, settling into the chair across from him. Maud took the seat beside me, her knitting bag resting in her lap though she made no move to take out her work.

'Then ask them.' He took a sip of his drink. 'I'm tired of pretending, Mrs Miller. Tired of watching my back and wondering who knows what. I had the most terrible argument with Stan because he wanted me to stop my illegal activities. I, on the other hand, was afraid I would lose my brother's respect if he found out what I'd been doing. It turns out he had been aware of my activities for some time.'

'You must have been furious with Stan.'

'It's a little hard to be angry with a dead man, Mrs Miller.'

I frowned. 'What do you mean?'

'Up until this morning, I believed my brother was in the dark about what I'd been doing. Of course, I was rather cross with Stan that he used telling my brother as a reason for me to stop what I was doing when he'd already told him.'

'But I assume you were still unhappy with Stan that he interfered in your private business and was badgering you to stop or come clean?'

'I was, yes.' He gave a small self-deprecating smile. 'I can imagine what you are going to ask me next: was I angry enough with Stan to kill him? Well, the answer to that, Mrs Miller, is no. He helped me with my debts, and I was grateful to him.'

I raised a disbelieving eyebrow. 'Why did you say that you hoped Stan was ready for the consequences of his interference?'

'Gosh.' Bernard stared at me as though he couldn't quite believe I was repeating his own words back to him. 'I did say that. But not in the manner I think you're inferring. It wasn't a threat. At least, I wasn't threatening Stan with harm. I was trying to make it clear to him that the consequences of him telling Ted would be a fracturing in the relationship between me and my brother. I didn't want that, or for Ted to be disappointed in me.'

'Then today you found out he knew all along,' I said gently, feeling rather sorry for Bernard despite his wrongdoing. 'Your brother is very worried about you.'

'My brother is a fool,' Bernard said, but there was more sadness than anger in his voice. 'A kind, loyal fool who deserves better than a brother who's brought shame to the family name.'

'Mr Harland, I need to ask you directly: where were you last night when I was attacked?'

He met my gaze steadily. 'I went out for a walk. I believed then, of course, that Stan's death meant Ted didn't know about what I'd been doing. I felt relieved, but also conflicted because even though it was beneficial to me, I never wanted harm to come to Stan.'

'You were by yourself?'

'For a time,' Bernard said. 'Then I saw lights on in the solicitor's office. I thought the fellow rather owed someone a favour, and so I thought to ask him for some legal advice.'

'You spoke to him?' I couldn't keep the surprise from my voice.

'I did,' Bernard confirmed. 'I told him everything. You

wouldn't understand, but goodness me, the burden felt lighter simply by sharing it with a stranger.'

'Did he give you advice on the best way forward for you?'

Bernard gave a hollow laugh. 'Even though it was past eleven o'clock, and we both know he hasn't always been very diligent in his legal practice, he did. He said I had a couple of options. The first one is more palatable: go back to Brighton, destroy the prescription pad, and carry on my business ethically and lawfully. The second is to confess to the police and let them deal with me.'

'However did it start?' Maud asked as she shook her head, though her voice was not accusatory. 'Selling prescription medication to those lost in their own addiction is a quite wicked thing to do.'

'I know,' he said, staring into his glass. 'It started small to cover a gambling debt. Stupid, really, betting on horses as though I were Lord Derby himself. Before I knew it, I was in deep, and the only way out seemed to be to expand my... services.'

'How did Stan find out?'

'He realised I never had two pennies to rub together, despite owning a seemingly prosperous pharmacy. He offered to help me with my finances. It didn't take long for him to realise where my money was going.' Bernard finished his drink, as though needing the alcohol to give him the courage to go on. 'He took the pharmacy accounts to look at cost-cutting measures and somehow the prescription pad was amongst the things he took. Of course, there's no good reason for a pharmacist to have one of those.'

'Despite Stan knowing all of your secrets, you didn't kill him?' I pressed.

The words hung in the air between us. Bernard's face had gone very pale. 'Good God, no! Is that what you really think, Mrs Miller? That I killed Stan?'

'You have to admit, you have a very good reason to want him dead. As you've just admitted, your choices are keep quiet or come clean and face ruin. Stan wasn't going to let you choose the first option, and now he's no longer here, you can carry on as you were doing.'

'No, he was trying to help me. I know it looks bad for me. But honestly, it's a relief to have it all out in the open. I feel as though I've been given a chance to turn my life around.'

'It's rather fortunate for you, then, that Stan's death allows that to be possible.'

'It's the truth,' he said wearily. 'Though I can quite clearly see why you wouldn't believe me. I have the knowledge of poisons, I had a motive, and I was in the village when it happened. But I swear to you, I did not kill Stan. He was my brother's dearest friend, as well as being a jolly good pal to me too.'

There was such anguish in his voice, such apparent sincerity, that I found myself wavering. Either Bernard Harland was an exceptional actor, or he was telling the truth.

Maud eyed him shrewdly. 'How did you know he was poisoned?'

'My dear lady,' Bernard said. 'I'm a pharmacist. It's quite clear to me from everything I know about Stan's death that he was poisoned. I'm as certain as I can be that the poison used was monkshood. Likely the poison was made into a paste and put inside his cricket gloves and then absorbed into his skin. The poor man never stood a chance.'

There didn't seem much more to say after that. Bernard Harland had set out all of the reasons he looked exceedingly guilty much better than we could.

'Well,' Maud said as we walked back to my cottage. 'What do you make of all that?'

'I don't know,' I admitted. 'He seemed genuine, but then, he's a man who's been lying and deceiving people for months. Why should we believe him now?'

'Perhaps because he has nothing left to lose by telling the truth?' Maud suggested. 'Or, equally, perhaps his remorse is an elaborate performance designed to throw us off the scent.'

Even as Maud said what I'd been thinking, doubt crept in. Bernard's confession, and his obvious distress, seemed so genuine. If he truly had killed Stan and attacked me, surely he would have been more defensive, more guarded, and come up with a much better alibi for the time I was attacked.

'I don't know what to think,' I admitted.

'Martha,' Maud said gently as she reached out and touched my arm, 'you look absolutely done in. Perhaps we should call it a day and you should spend the rest of the day resting.'

'I can't rest,' I said, touching my bandaged head. 'Someone in this village is a murderer, Maud. Someone killed my husband, and then tried to kill me. Every hour we delay is another hour they have to cover their tracks. Not to mention Ben has suggested delaying the wedding. We both know that's not what Ruby wants.'

'Martha Miller, you're no good to anyone if you collapse from exhaustion. You've spoken to nearly every suspect, and no doubt learned more than the police, all with a head injury that would have most people lying in bed. You must be sensible. I insist you go home, rest, and think things through quietly. Perhaps the answer will come to you when you're not chasing it so frantically.'

I wanted to argue, to insist that I needed to continue, to speak with Walter Preston, and Oliver Beckwith, and hopefully uncover the final piece of evidence that would reveal the killer's identity. But Maud had a good point; I needed to rest. The throbbing in my head had intensified, and a wave of dizziness made me sway slightly on my feet.

'Perhaps you're right,' I conceded.

As we walked back through the village, I couldn't shake the feeling that I was missing something crucial. All the pieces were there – the motives, the means, the opportunities – but they weren't fitting together the way they should. It was like trying to complete a jigsaw puzzle with pieces from multiple boxes, none of them quite matching up to create a clear picture.

12

'Do stay for dinner, Mrs Burnett,' Ruby said as she met us at the garden gate.

'Oh no, my dear, I don't want to intrude on a family meal.' Maud shot me a pleading look.

'Nonsense,' I said. 'You are family, Mrs Burnett. I insist that you join us.'

As we entered the house together, the smell from the kitchen surprised me. Usually, when Ruby spent time cooking, the air carried a faint whiff of burning; steam would billow around the room as if we were standing on the platform when a train pulled in, and the vegetables had been boiled so thoroughly one needed a spoon with which to eat them.

'Dinner smells wonderful, doesn't it?' Ben asked as we entered the kitchen.

It did.

I wanted to ask who had made it, but the beaming smile on my sister's face stopped me from saying anything. 'Yes, it does. Well done, Ruby.'

I went over to the Aga and lifted the lid of the gently simmering pot. Without asking, I knew the answer to my unasked question: without a doubt, the cookware belonged to Ada Bennington.

Maud peeked over my shoulder. 'Mmm, rabbit stew. It looks wonderful, dear.'

'Glad you were persuaded to stay now, aren't you?' Ruby gave Maud a saucy wink. 'I thought Friday's leftover bread would go well with it.'

She was right. Only dunking would make the shop-bought loaf soft enough to eat. I'd bought it on Friday, but heaven knows when it had been baked. I longed for the day I could walk into the village shop and find what I needed without the infernal ration books.

Dinner was delicious – I made a mental note to thank Ada for helping out. I could probably do that when I returned her pot. Ruby was back at work in the morning, her final week of work before her marriage. Although Ruby was a fairly modern woman by anyone's standards, not even she intended to stay at work after she married Ben.

That was, if the wedding went ahead, after Ben's comment about postponing it given the circumstances. I really needed to give some thought to Stan's funeral. No doubt Ted and Bernard, police allowing, would be returning to Brighton as soon as they could. It was something I hadn't considered before that moment – suspects would not stay in Westleham to wait for the murderer to be uncovered.

Buses did not run on a Sunday in Westleham, but there would be two buses travelling to Winteringham the next day – no doubt Annie and Lavinia intended to be on one of them.

'What's next for you, Martha?' Ben asked as though he could read my mind.

'I need to speak to Walter Preston again,' I said. 'Then Oliver Beckwith.'

'You do not,' Maud retorted. 'You need to sit down and relax. Your face is as white as your bandage.'

'I feel fine.'

'Well, you do not look fine,' she huffed.

It was rather nice to have someone who cared about my well-being. It wasn't that my parents didn't care – only that there were so many of us, and we'd been brought up on the rule that if you weren't bleeding or dying there was no use making a fuss about whatever ailed you.

'Come along,' he said. 'I shall go with you.'

'Really? Won't Detective Inspector Kennington have something to say about that?'

Ben shrugged. 'I'm simply taking a walk through the village with my soon-to-be sister-in-law. Besides, someone is extremely keen to have the murderer caught so there can be a wedding next weekend.'

Ruby flushed. 'It's all organised, Ben. Invites went out weeks ago; it would be awfully difficult to cancel or rearrange it at such short notice.'

'I'm teasing,' he said. 'I only mentioned it in case anyone thought it was in bad taste to have a wedding so soon after Stan's death.'

'It perhaps would be had Stan and I loved each other as ordinary married couples do,' I said sadly. 'But we all know that isn't the case, and it's pointless to pretend otherwise.'

'Though you must bear in mind we live in a small village, dear,' Maud said with a note of caution in her voice. 'It would be most unseemly if the vicar rushed through the burial and was walking out with the widow the following week. People would talk.'

After years in Westleham, I understood only too well how damaging the gossipmongering could be. When Stan first went missing, many of the villagers had been convinced that he was buried underneath the potato patch in our back garden.

'Perhaps it would be better to bury Stan after the wedding,' I said. 'Even if his body is released before then. There's sure to be an inquest, so it would make sense.'

'That would be sensible, dear.' Maud nodded her agreement. 'And be sure to continue as you currently do with the vicar. People will need to see a decent period of mourning, even when the murderer is caught and it isn't Luke.'

'Of course it isn't Luke,' Ruby said. 'It's ridiculous that people would ever think such a thing.'

'And yet they will.' Maud got to her feet. 'Now, if you do not need me for sleuthing duty this afternoon, I think I shall go home and take a nap. Thank you so much for including me in your family meal.'

On impulse, I got up too and crossed the room towards my neighbour. To her astonishment, I bent slightly and kissed her cheek. 'Thank you, Maud.'

'What was that for?' she asked, pressing two fingers to her cheek.

I lifted a shoulder, a little embarrassed at my own spontaneity. 'Just a little thank you for all you do so that you know you're appreciated.'

'Goodness me, dear,' Maud said in her usual no-nonsense way. 'Isn't that what neighbours are for?'

I'm not sure when it happened, only that it did: Maud stopped being just my neighbour. She became a dear friend – more than that, the granny Ruby and I had needed as children but hadn't had. I was so grateful to have that now.

* * *

Ruby insisted Ben and I leave immediately to visit Walter Preston. I felt guilty leaving her with the washing up, but Ben reminded me that part of the reason I was pushing myself so hard to find Stan's killer was so the wedding could go ahead as planned.

We walked left out of my garden and towards the Bennington farm. Walter Preston's somewhat grand house, The Limes, was on the right at the edge of the village.

Ben used the sparkling brass door knocker to announce our presence in the way only policemen can do. As is usual in a small village on a Sunday afternoon, the door was answered quickly. However, not by either of the house owners but by a rather harried-looking maid.

'May we speak to Mr Preston?' Ben asked in a commanding voice.

'Of course.' The maid practically bobbed her knee at Ben as she stood back and allowed us entry to the house. 'I'll let him know you're here.'

I had never visited the house when the Carters lived there, but it was extremely doubtful that they favoured the sort of ostentatious show of wealth The Limes exuded now. Walking along the corridor, I stopped to admire a painting on the wall. I knew nothing of art work, but I knew what I did and didn't like and this painting was hideous.

'Wonderful, isn't it, Mrs Miller?' Walter Preston practically preened as he came out of a room I assumed was the drawing room.

'I have no words,' I told him honestly.

'You'd better come in,' he said, extending an arm towards the room he'd come from. 'Then I can tell you what I've already told Detective Inspector Kennington.'

He showed us into a room that was over furnished and under lit. It gave the impression of stepping into some sort of Aladdin's Cave.

'Refreshments, sir?' the maid asked from the door, as though she was afraid to step over the threshold into the cluttered room.

'No thank you, Mabel, I don't think my guests will be staying long enough.'

'I suppose I will have to leave again?'

The voice came from near my elbow and I looked down to see Cynthia Preston lounging on a sofa clad in the sort of outfit that would be more at home in a bride's trousseau than worn at home on a Sunday afternoon. Though, of course, what did I know of fashion? What I knew about the clothing normal wives wore in their own homes I could easily write on the back of a postage stamp.

'I'm afraid so. Sorry, my dear.' Unlike his words, Walter Preston's tone contained no apology.

With a swish of pink silk satin, Cynthia Preston sashayed her way out of the room. If I wasn't very much mistaken, Walter Preston would need to find someone else to help with his business deals if he wanted to raise enough money to keep his wife happy.

'I want to ask you specifically about where you were last night,' Ben said without preamble.

'Here at home,' Walter answered promptly.

'You didn't leave for any reason?'

It was actually rather relaxing to have someone else ask all the questions. It also allowed me to watch Walter Preston's face more clearly as he spoke to Ben. The mild irritation had an obvious origin – he had told Ben he wanted to repeat what he'd already told the other detective, but Ben had his own agenda.

'I did not.'

'You didn't, for instance, walk up the lane while having a late-night cigar?'

'Absolutely not.' Walter Preston shook his head decisively. 'Cynthia hates the smell of cigars so insists I stand outside when I'm smoking. Can you believe that? She sends her own husband out of his own house in all weathers. I don't know what the world is coming to when women think they can insist on things like that.'

Clearly Walter Preston, despite his bluster, did not wear the trousers in this house. It amused me to think of petite Cynthia Preston demanding her much larger husband did as she asked.

'Shocking,' Ben said in an even voice that indicated none of the amusement I was certain he was feeling.

'Occasionally, I sit in the gardener's shed.' Walter Preston paused so long after this statement that I couldn't help but wonder if his words were supposed to mean something to me.

'How dreadful for you,' Ben murmured. 'I assume that has some relevance?'

'It does,' Walter Preston said as excitement suffused his face. 'When I went into the shed this morning before church, I discovered the gardening gloves I keep there were missing.'

'When did you last use them?'

'He doesn't use them,' I said. 'Frank Bennington does the garden here.'

'Well, yes,' he admitted. 'But they were there, and now they're not.'

'Perhaps young Frank moved them?'

'He didn't,' the business owner said smugly as though he had got one over on Ben. 'I checked with him this morning. I specifically asked him to use his own gloves when he touched those poisonous plants so I would've been most vexed to find he'd used my gloves. He insisted he hadn't touched them and they should still be in the shed.'

'How long ago did Frank plant the monkshood?'

'I couldn't say precisely.' Walter Preston shifted in his seat, looking decidedly uncomfortable for the first time since he invited us to sit down in his drawing room. 'A week or so ago possibly. Probably best to check with the farmer's lad. He'll know better than me.'

'Do you keep the shed locked?' I asked.

'Whatever for?' He looked at me as though I was mad and had just suggested water wasn't wet. 'There's nothing of value in there – just a few old tools, some clay pots, that sort of thing. Anyone could have walked in and taken the gloves.'

'How convenient,' I murmured.

Preston's jaw tightened. 'Now see here, Mrs Miller. I know what you're implying, but I had nothing to do with your husband's death. Yes, Stan and I had our... disagreements, but I certainly didn't kill him over them.'

'How long were you outside?' Ben asked.

Walter frowned at me, then looked at Ben, the look of confusion not clearing. 'When?'

'Last night,' Ben clarified with exaggerated patience. 'When your wife insisted you go outside to smoke your cigar instead of allowing you to enjoy it in your own home.'

I forced my expression to remain neutral though inside I longed to laugh out loud at the way Ben had thrown Preston's words back at him.

He stared at Ben for a moment, unsure how to take Ben's words before deciding the detective was clearly on his side. 'I suppose around ten minutes or so. However long it took me to smoke my cigar.'

'Did you see anyone?'

Preston shook his head emphatically. 'No, I did not. I didn't see... Oh, wait, I did see someone. That farmer's lad. Do you think he waited until I went inside before taking the gloves?'

His lack of awareness was stunning, though it shouldn't have surprised me. Men with money and a sense of their own 'position' seldom notice other people's lives unless those lives touch their own.

'Although it's undoubtedly of great interest to the investigation that someone took gardening gloves out of your shed, we're here to talk to you about your movements last night.' Ben gestured at the bandage covering my head. 'Specifically where you were at the time Mrs Miller was assaulted.'

'Oh no!' Walter Preston held his hands out in front of him as though he thought he was about to be physically attacked. 'That's too far, Detective Inspector. I would never hurt a woman. I admit my business dealings sometimes run a fine line between above board and, shall we say, imaginative, but no one ever gets hurt.'

'Not physically hurt, anyway,' I cut in. 'I can't imagine that the Carters were very happy to lose this beautiful house.'

'I bought it from them fair and square,' he insisted.

'I don't think anything about the house purchase was fair.' I couldn't help but feel very cross that this man had something over Stan that had caused him to pass on details of the Carters' poor financial state to Walter Preston. 'You blackmailed Stan into giving you the Carters' personal banking information.'

'Blackmail is such an ugly word, Mrs Miller.' He inspected his fingernails. 'Anyway, we've already had this conversation. I was introduced to the Carters and paid the price they asked.'

'Blackmail is exactly what it was.' There was a steel in Ben's voice that I rarely heard, and it reminded me that he had achieved his rank because he was an extremely good policeman.

But there was something else in his tone and it took me a moment to realise what the emotion was – disgust. Of course, blackmail was a horrible act, but it was more than that.

'You know.' I breathed. 'You know what he had over Stan, don't you?'

Ben looked at me with sadness. 'It has no relevance to the investigation.'

'Perhaps not.' I swallowed. 'But it matters to me.'

'I told you before,' Walter said. 'It's not a topic fit for your ears.'

'He was my husband!' I had suddenly had enough of the businessman's oily personality. 'I demand that you tell me immediately.'

'No, Martha.' Ben put a hand on my arm. 'On this occasion, Mr Preston is correct. You don't want to know.'

'And I am telling you that I do,' I insisted quietly. 'Now, which of you will tell me?'

Ben looked down at the floor, his cheeks red. 'If you insist, I shall tell you.'

'I insist.' Even as I said the words, I wondered if I really wanted to hear them. Ben's demeanour told me that he really didn't want to share the information with me, so I knew it would be difficult to hear. Yet after everything that had happened over the last few days, I wanted to know. Perhaps it would help me understand my husband better.

'I learned what I am going to tell you from Detective Inspector Kennington. He immediately realised it must have been the reason Stan did what Preston asked of him despite it being against everything we knew about his integrity.'

'Integrity.' Walter Preston didn't even try and hide his snigger.

'Please, just tell me.'

'Mr Preston discovered that Stan was involved with a man,' Ben said in a tight voice, as though every word was being dragged out of him. 'In a romantic relationship.'

'Stan?' I asked in disbelief, but even as I said it, my incredulity melted away. Suddenly, after years of sadness and confusion, my entire marriage made perfect sense.

'I'm so sorry, Martha.' Ben looked at me in sorrow. 'I never wanted you to find out, and certainly not like this.'

I turned to Walter Preston. 'And because you knew that about my husband, you forced him to do something against his will?'

'A man like that clearly has no ethics, so I encouraged him to help me in a few business transactions.'

Rage boiled through me, and it took everything I had to make my voice calm and reasonable. 'Do we need to ask Mr Preston anything else?'

'I think that's everything.' Ben got to his feet and, I'm sure, didn't miss the look of relief on Walter Preston's face.

No sooner had the front door closed behind us than Ben apologised again. I held up a hand. 'Out of respect for Stan, and the life he chose to lead, let's never speak of this again. It has no bearing on the case.'

'No, it doesn't,' Ben agreed.

We walked in silence as I processed the revelation. Although it was new information, there was something familiar about it. Almost as if I had always known, somewhere deep inside. It was rather shocking to hear the words said out loud, of course, but instead of feeling angry at Stan, I felt unspeakably sad for him. How awful for him to have been so unhappy in our marriage, and be unable to tell me the truth. In a strange way, it also made me feel free. It wouldn't have mattered what I'd done, or how hard I tried, I would never have been the spouse that Stan wanted.

As we walked away from Preston's house, I put the news about Stan to the back of my mind and mulled over what Walter Preston had told us – the missing gardening gloves were an interesting development.

'What do you think about the gloves?' I asked Ben.

'I think someone is being very clever,' he replied. 'Either Preston killed Stan and is now trying to make it look like someone else used his gloves and his monkshood, or someone else is framing him rather effectively.'

'The missing gloves certainly complicate things.'

'Indeed. And with no lock on the shed, anyone in the village could have taken them.' Ben sighed. 'This case is like trying to knit fog, Martha. Every time I think I've got hold of something solid, it slips through my fingers.'

* * *

We walked back towards the village and towards Oliver Beckwith's house. Even though he had been in his office the night before, neither of us could imagine that we would find him there on a Sunday afternoon.

Ben rapped firmly on the door. After a moment's pause, we heard the tap of a stick and shuffling footsteps before the scrape of a bolt being drawn back.

Oliver opened the door, his face registering surprise when he saw us. 'Detective Inspector Robertson. Mrs Miller.' He glanced nervously between us. 'I wasn't expecting visitors on a Sunday afternoon.'

'We won't take much of your time, Mr Beckwith,' Ben said pleasantly. 'Just a few questions, if you don't mind.'

'Of course, of course. Come in.' He stood back to let us enter, though his reluctance was palpable.

'How is your injury?' I asked, more from politeness than genuine concern.

He led us down a long hallway into an imposing room that he clearly used as a home office. The fact that he had such a functional room in his house made it even more perplexing that he would choose to go to his offices the evening before – particularly taking into account his injured ankle.

'Improving, thank you. Dr Briggs says I should be able to walk without the stick in another week or so.' He sat behind an imposing desk, swung his legs to the side, and rested his ankle on a footstool placed for his comfort. 'Now, what can I help you with?'

'We're gathering information on where everyone in the village was late last night. Nothing official, you understand, but we'd appreciate your cooperation – especially if you can help us identify the person who attacked Mrs Miller in such a cowardly way. I understand your office lights were on quite late – past eleven o'clock. Can you tell us why?'

A flush crept up Oliver's neck. 'I... well, yes. I was working late on some urgent matters.'

'Urgent matters on a Saturday night?' Ben's tone remained polite, but there was an edge of scepticism.

'Client confidentiality prevents me from discussing specifics, but yes, occasionally legal work requires attention outside of normal business hours.'

'Wouldn't it have been more comfortable for someone to bring the files you required to your home?' I looked around the room with deliberate slowness. 'You seem rather well set up here.'

'If only it were that simple, my dear lady,' he said with a

simpering tone. I wasn't about to be taken in by any attempt of his to be pleasant. I had asked about his injury, but he had not asked about mine. He was a thoroughly unpleasant man. 'It would have taken so long for my wife to have located the correct papers, it was easier to go myself.'

'Goodness,' I said. 'Perhaps you should consider a better filing system. Losing paperwork – and committing such a serious clerical error that meant I never received maintenance paid for my express benefit – doesn't seem like the best way to run a solicitor's firm.'

'Well, really!' He huffed. 'How very rude.'

'Mr Beckwith,' Ben said. 'Let me be plain: Mrs Miller's missing maintenance money isn't the only concern the police have with your business practices.'

'It's not missing,' he blustered. 'I gave Mrs Miller a cheque yesterday. For the full amount.'

'Be that as it may,' Ben said. 'I would hope you were not destroying evidence of your misdeeds last night.'

'What a scurrilous allegation!' Oliver managed to sound outraged, as though the allegation was utterly preposterous.

'No doubt that investigation will continue tomorrow.' Ben leaned forward. 'Today, however, I'm more interested in Mr Miller's murder and the attack late last night on Mrs Miller. Were you alone last night?'

The solicitor paused, clearly weighing up his options before answering. 'I was on my own for a considerable length of time before a member of the public came by asking for legal advice.'

'Did that person engage your services?'

'He did not.'

'In that case, we can proceed on the understanding that client confidentiality does not exist between you and your late-night visitor. Moving along, can you tell me what you discussed?'

'Bernard Harland saw my light on and stopped by for advice' – Oliver's voice dropped to barely above a whisper – 'for a very delicate matter.'

'What time did he arrive?'

'Just after eleven. I know the time fairly accurately as I glanced at the clock before going to the door.'

'And how long did he stay?'

'Perhaps half an hour. Maybe a little longer.' Oliver shifted in his seat again, this time from discomfort that had nothing to do with his ankle. 'He was very distressed. Wanted to know his options regarding certain business practices that might not have been entirely... above board.'

'Did he tell you what those practices were?' I asked.

Oliver hesitated, clearly torn between professional discretion and the gravity of a murder investigation. 'He mentioned something about prescription medications. I advised him that his best course of action was to cease any questionable activities immediately and seek legal counsel as soon as he got back to Brighton.'

'You didn't offer to represent him yourself?' Ben asked.

'Good heavens, no. I'm a country solicitor, Detective Inspector. I handle wills, property transactions, that sort of thing. Criminal law is well outside my expertise. No, a solicitor who lives in his home town is a much better solution for both of us.'

'After Mr Harland left, what did you do?' Ben asked. 'Presumably it was around half past eleven then, as you've said he stayed around half an hour.'

'I finished up my work – which didn't take long, perhaps another fifteen minutes – then locked up and went home. My wife was already in bed, but she can confirm what time I returned. It was just before midnight.'

Ben paused while he digested what the solicitor had told him. 'Mr Beckwith, I need to ask you directly: did you have any involvement in the death of Stan Miller or the attack on Mrs Miller?'

'Absolutely not!' Oliver's voice rose indignantly. 'Yes, I made mistakes with Mrs Miller's maintenance payments – mistakes I deeply regret and have attempted to rectify. But I'm not a violent man, Detective Inspector. As I've just said: I'm a humble country solicitor, for heaven's sake!'

'A solicitor who embezzled money from a client,' I pointed out, unable to keep the bitterness from my voice. 'I'm sure there are many solicitors who would do what they could to prevent that knowledge from tainting your firm's reputation.'

Oliver's face went from red to ashen. 'I... That's a very harsh way of putting it, Mrs Miller.'

'Is there a gentler word for taking money that wasn't yours?'

'As I've told you several times now, it was a simple clerical error,' he said stiffly.

'Did you see or notice anything unusual on your way home?' Ben asked.

'No.' He shook his head and then a thought seemed to occur to him. 'Everything seemed quiet, as usual, but as I neared my house I heard a dog barking. Not unusual, of course, but it was unusual at that time of night.'

Bless Lizzy, who had barked loudly enough to wake both Maud and Ruby so they could come to my aid. Otherwise, goodness only knew how long I would've lain in the back garden.

'What about yesterday morning?' Ben enquired. 'When I visited your house, you were barely able to hobble around, but by last night you were well enough to go over to your office to complete urgent paperwork.'

'What's the question?' The solicitor's tone could only be described as surly.

'It seemed to me that you were quite incapacitated yesterday morning, but by late last night, your recovery was quite miraculous. It's possible, is it not, that you went over to the cricket green and tampered with Mr Miller's cricket gloves, and were back home before I arrived.'

'Are you suggesting I faked my injury?' Oliver asked, outrage causing his face to turn an alarming shade of red. 'Because I can assure you that Dr Briggs said that my ankle is badly sprained.'

'I would like you to answer my question.'

'Of course I didn't go over to the cricket green. I didn't leave the house all day. I was in a lot of pain.' At Ben's pointed look, he amended his words. 'That is, until I went to my office late last night.'

No doubt Oliver Beckwith's wife would confirm his alibi – whether or not he had left home yesterday. That didn't necessarily rule him out for my attack. He could have made up the 'memory' of a dog barking to make his story seem authentic.

As Ben had said, it was like trying to nail jelly to a wall – every time we learned something new, something else didn't fit, and we seemed to be no nearer to finding the killer.

'Thank you, Mr Beckwith.' Ben gave me a nod and we left the solicitor's house. 'What do you think?'

'I think Oliver Beckwith is a weasel who stole my money, but I'm not sure he's a murderer,' I admitted. 'It would have taken time for him to limp over to the cricket ground, and you would think he would've been spotted. It's rather hard to be furtive with a walking stick.'

We walked in silence for a moment, the evening air cool against my face. My head had begun to throb again – a reminder that Dr Briggs had been right about my need for rest.

'Martha,' Ben said quietly, 'I know you're determined to solve this case, but you really do need to be careful. Whoever killed

Stan and attacked you is still out there, and they're clearly desperate enough to be dangerous.'

'I know,' I said. 'But the wedding is in six days, Ben. I can't let this drag on and ruin Ruby's special day.'

'The wedding won't be ruined,' he assured me. 'Ruby and I will be married regardless of whether the murderer is caught by then. I give you my word that I won't delay it, but I'd rather have you alive to attend than have you laid up in hospital – or worse – because you pushed yourself too hard.'

His concern touched me. 'I promise I'll be careful.'

'Good. Because Ruby would never forgive me if something happened to you.' We reached my gate, and Ben gave me a gentle reminder to lock all my doors and windows. As I watched him walk back down the lane toward the middle of the village, in the direction of the cottage he would soon share with Ruby, I couldn't help but feel the investigation was closing in on its conclusion. All the pieces were there – I just needed to fit them together properly.

13

Inside, I found Ruby and Maud in the parlour, the wireless playing softly in the background. They both looked up expectantly as I entered.

'Well?' Ruby asked. 'What did you learn?'

I sank into my favourite chair with a sigh. 'That Bernard Harland was at Oliver Beckwith's office, as Bernard claimed. Ben and I agree that Oliver would have struggled to kill either Stan or me, due to his injured ankle. Meanwhile Walter Preston's gardening gloves have mysteriously gone missing. Finally, it seems that I have far too many suspects who all had motive, means, and opportunity.'

'But surely some can be eliminated now?' Maud asked, her knitting needles pausing mid-stitch.

'Oliver looks unlikely. Theoretically he could have attacked Stan but he's heavily reliant on his stick. I can't see him getting into the pavilion without being seen – he would be so conspicuous. Additionally, because of his injury, I just don't see him being able to hit me with any amount of force.'

Maud chuckled. 'No, he probably would have toppled over.'

I smiled. It felt nice to have a moment of levity given we were discussing someone attacking me in my garden – a place where I should have felt safe.

'What about Walter Preston?' Ruby asked.

'He certainly could have committed either crime. The gardening gloves have been taken from his shed which he says is never locked, and he can't be sure when they were taken, only that the last time they were used was when Frank planted the monkshood.'

Maud shuddered. 'I don't like that man. He's so arrogant, and taking advantage of the Carters the way he did is just wicked.'

'Ben thinks someone might be trying to frame him.'

'You don't sound so sure,' Maud said.

'There was something about the way he reacted when Ben asked him where he was at the time I was attacked. He was horrified. No, more than that – disgusted that anyone could attack a woman.'

'A man like that lies for a living.' Maud shook her head. 'You shouldn't allow yourself to be taken in by a serial liar, Martha.'

'Is Bernard Harland still in the frame?' Ruby asked.

'Definitely,' I said. 'As I've said, Oliver confirmed that he was at his offices with him. There wasn't much time for him to leave, hit me, and get back to the pub but yes, I think it's possible. Also, he has a very solid motive for wanting Stan out of the way.'

'Hmm.' Maud put her knitting in her lap. 'Hear me out while I work through this theory that has just come to me. Is it possible that the reason you were only hit once is because whoever did it was rushing? Maybe if he thought he had more time, he would have done a more thorough job.'

'Gosh, what a heartwarming thought, Maud!' Ruby looked at me in concern.

'It's a good point,' I said. 'Until now, I thought the reason I was hit was to stop me investigating, to scare me off. It's definitely possible my attacker simply didn't have the time to cause the harm they intended.'

It was a sobering thought, but I was glad that Maud had raised the possibility. It was important that I look at all angles, no matter how unpalatable they may be.

Maud resumed her knitting. 'What about Ted Harland?'

'No alibi for the attack on me – he claims he was in his room at the pub. And he had as much reason as his brother to want Stan silenced, perhaps more so given his loyalty to Bernard.'

'And Lavinia Thompson?'

I rubbed my temples, trying to ease the persistent ache. 'Also no proper alibi. She claims she was at the church praying, but that's completely unverifiable.'

Ruby leaned forward. 'Martha, has it occurred to you that the person who attacked you might not be the same person who killed Stan?'

Maud and I both looked at her in surprise.

'What do you mean?' I asked.

'Well, think about it. Stan's murder was carefully planned – the poison had to be prepared, the gloves had to be treated without anyone noticing, the timing had to be perfect. It required knowledge of poisons and access to the pavilion. But the attack on you was rather... improvised, wasn't it? Someone grabbed a branch and hit you with it. That's not the same level of planning at all.'

I sat back, considering her words. Ruby was right – the two attacks had very different characteristics. Stan's murder had been methodical and calculated. My attack had been opportunistic and crude.

'But surely it's too much of a coincidence for them not to be connected,' Maud objected. 'Martha was attacked the same day she began investigating Stan's death.'

'I'm not saying they're not connected,' Ruby clarified. 'I'm saying perhaps there's more than one person involved. Or perhaps the murderer was desperate to stop Martha but didn't have time to plan something more sophisticated.'

'Or,' I said slowly, 'the person who attacked me wanted to frighten me off the investigation but didn't actually want to kill me. If they'd wanted me dead, they could have hit me multiple times while I was unconscious.'

A heavy silence fell over the room as we all considered the implications. If the attacker had shown restraint – mercy, even – what did that tell us about their identity?

'Surely anyone who was desperate enough to kill Stan wouldn't hesitate to kill you if they thought you were getting close to the truth?' Maud asked.

'Unless they killed Stan in the heat of the moment and then regretted it,' Ruby suggested. 'Perhaps, as you believed, attacking you was meant as a warning, not an attempt at murder.'

My head was spinning, and not just from the injury. Every time I thought I understood what had happened, a new angle presented itself that called everything into question.

I thought about Ruby's insight regarding the difference between Stan's murder and my attack. She was right – they had very different characteristics. Stan's death had been calculated and clever. My attack had been crude and desperate.

Perhaps her observation held more weight than I'd realised, and they weren't meant to achieve the same goal. Stan's murder had been meant to silence him permanently. My attack had been meant to frighten me away from the investigation.

Which suggested the murderer wasn't quite as ruthless as I'd imagined. They'd killed Stan because they believed they had to –

because whatever secret he threatened to expose was worth murder to protect. But they didn't want to kill again unless absolutely necessary.

That was something, at least. It meant I had a chance to solve this before anyone else died.

'I think,' I said finally, 'I need to do what Maud suggested earlier. I need to stop chasing the answers and let them come to me. Perhaps if I review everything I know – all the conversations, all the evidence, all the little details – the pattern will become clear.'

'A good night's sleep wouldn't hurt either,' Maud added pointedly. 'You look absolutely done in, dear.'

She was right, of course. The combination of the head injury, the emotional strain, and the constant activity since Stan's death had left me exhausted. Perhaps in the morning, with a clear head, I would finally see what I'd been missing all along.

However, I was reluctant to give up, especially not at six o'clock in the evening. I had a few hours before bedtime. 'Would anyone like supper?'

Maud patted her stomach. 'Not for me, thank you. I'm still full after that feast Ruby served up for dinner.'

'I might make a cup of cocoa and go to bed,' Ruby said. 'I know it's early, but I didn't sleep much last night after your attack. Now you're home and safe, I think an early night might do me some good.'

'That's a jolly good idea,' Maud said. 'Get in as much rest as you can, while you can.'

Ruby didn't react to Maud's cryptic quip. 'Cup of tea, Maud?'

'Wonderful idea, I'm parched.'

I followed Ruby into the kitchen, not because I wanted a drink, but because I wanted to go back through the notes I'd left on the kitchen table.

* * *

I was spreading my notes in front of me when I heard a knock at the front door. Ruby had just put the kettle on and was reaching for cups.

'I'll get it,' I said. I was keen to add the new knowledge to my notes and see if I could see a pattern, but it wouldn't hurt to give my mind another few minutes to think things through.

To my surprise, Luke stood on the doorstep with Dr Briggs beside him. My heart gave an involuntary flutter at the sight of Luke, despite everything.

'Good evening, Mrs Miller,' Dr Briggs said warmly. 'I hope you don't mind us calling, I wanted to check on your head injury. As it happens, Mrs Briggs had made an apple pie she insisted I deliver to the vicarage. As soon as he knew where I was heading, the vicar insisted he accompany me.'

'Of course not, please come in.' I stepped aside to let them enter, acutely aware of my still-dramatic bandage and general dishevelled state. 'Ruby has just put the kettle on.'

'I thought I heard voices.' Maud came into the corridor. 'Ah, Doctor, Vicar. Good evening.'

'Good evening.' Dr Briggs took off his hat and hung it on the hall stand. 'Shall we go into the kitchen if your delightful sister is boiling the kettle?'

'Come along, Doctor,' Maud said as she stepped in front of me. 'Let's get you settled with a nice cup of tea, then you can check Mrs Miller's injury, though I'm afraid to tell you that she has not been resting as you insisted she should.'

Luke and I shared a smile as Maud went into the kitchen behind the doctor, ensuring that we had a few moments alone. He reached out and touched his fingers to mine. 'How are you? Any investigative progress?'

'I'm all right. Truly, I am. A little headache, but all things considered, it could have been a lot worse. The investigation is jolly tricky, I must say. How are you?'

'Detective Inspector Kennington has grilled me several times.' Luke grimaced. 'I think I've convinced him I had nothing to do with Stan's death but as is typical for Westleham, someone has been whispering in his ear that I spend too much time unsupervised with you.'

'That isn't true!' I covered my cheeks with my hands. 'But I bet I can guess who told him that: Winnie Noble, without a doubt.'

'Mrs Miller, what on earth are you doing?' Maud called. 'The doctor wants to look at your head, and he can't do that while you are dilly-dallying in the corridor.'

Luke gave my fingers a squeeze before stepping back to follow me into the kitchen. I hoped my cheeks were not too pink – from either consternation at the village gossip, or from Luke's touch.

We settled around the kitchen table. After washing his hands, Dr Briggs unwound the bandage and examined my head wound with gentle efficiency, asking questions about pain levels, dizziness, and whether I'd experienced any nausea.

'I understand from Mrs Burnett that you haven't been following my advice.' He made a tsk-tsk noise, but gave me a kindly smile. 'Everything looks as it should, there's no fresh bleeding, so I think we can leave the bandage off. I'm afraid you'll have a scar, but it's mostly in your hairline so won't be very noticeable.'

I hadn't even considered that there might be a mark. 'Not very noticeable' to a doctor was not the same thing as not there. I immediately thought of what I would look like next week on

Ruby's wedding day – would there be bruising, or a lurid scar that would spoil the wedding pictures?

Ruby, as though knowing where my thoughts were, peered at my head. 'Your hat will cover that. Don't worry. No one will even know it's there.'

'You're very fortunate,' he said. 'A few inches to the side and you could've lost an eye. A more ferocious blow and we might be having a very different conversation.'

'Or not having one at all,' Maud added darkly.

'Goodness, Mrs Burnett,' Luke said. 'Let's not borrow trouble before it's due. Martha's had quite enough for one week.'

'That was quite a sermon this morning, Vicar,' Dr Briggs said, stirring sugar into his tea. 'Very stern stuff. It made me want to confess every sin I've ever committed. "Be sure your sin will find you out." Numbers 32:23, if I'm not mistaken?'

Luke nodded. 'I felt it was appropriate given current circumstances. Someone in our village has committed murder, and I believe that must weigh heavily on their conscience.'

'Do you really think murderers have consciences?' Maud asked sceptically.

'I believe everyone has a conscience, though some are better at silencing it than others.' Luke's gaze was distant, thoughtful. 'The burden of sin – especially one as grave as murder – is not easily borne. That's why confession is so important. The Lord forgives all sins, even murder, if true repentance is shown.'

Something in his words struck me oddly. I set down my teacup, my hand suddenly unsteady.

'Even murder?' I heard myself say. 'Do you truly believe that? Do you think others believe that, too?'

'Absolutely.' Luke's expression was earnest. 'God's mercy is infinite. No sin is beyond forgiveness if the sinner genuinely repents and seeks redemption. That's the very foundation of our faith – that Christ died for all our sins, not just the minor ones.'

'I know I'm going to heaven,' Maud stated with certainty. 'While I understand what you're saying, Vicar, I don't know that I want to share paradise with murderers and other fiends.'

I didn't hear Luke's reply as a strange sensation washed over me, as if puzzle pieces were suddenly shifting in my mind. Something about Luke's words – about forgiveness, about sin, about burden and conscience – was connecting with something else. Something I'd heard or observed but not fully processed.

'Martha?' Ruby's concerned voice seemed to come from very far away. 'Are you all right? You've gone ever so pale again.'

'I'm fine,' I managed, though I wasn't entirely sure that was true. My heart was racing, and my thoughts were tumbling over each other in a confused rush. 'Just a bit tired, I think.'

'Perhaps we should let you rest,' Dr Briggs said, already rising.

Luke stood too and looked down at me, concern etched across his handsome face. 'Did I say something to upset you?'

'Not at all,' I said quickly, rearranging my notes. 'It's strange – something you said sparked a thought, but it fluttered off before I could see what it was. Like a name on the tip of your tongue, there for a heartbeat and gone the next.'

'What did I say?' He frowned as he thought. 'Mercy. Sin. Forgiveness. Repentance. Redemption.'

'Yes.' I nodded. 'All of those things.'

It was no good; the more I tried to recall the memory, the quicker it flitted away.

The Lord forgives everyone their sins – even the murderer.

Why had those words affected me so profoundly? What was my subconscious trying to tell me?

'At the risk of repeating myself,' Dr Briggs said, 'rest is always the best thing in situations like this. You've had a blow to the head, Mrs Miller. It's not surprising your powers of recollection are not as sharp as normal.'

I stared down at my notes without really seeing them. Luke's words kept echoing in my mind, mingling with fragments of conversations I'd had over the past few days.

'Of course, Doctor,' I murmured.

True repentance... burden of sin... conscience... forgiveness...

And suddenly, with shocking clarity, I knew.

I knew who had killed Stan.

The knowledge settled over me like a weight – heavy, undeniable, and unspeakably sad. Now that I understood, I could see every clue I'd missed, every small inconsistency and odd behaviour that fell neatly into place when viewed through the right lens.

'Oh,' I whispered. 'Oh, no.'

'Oh no?' Dr Briggs repeated.

'She's got it,' Luke said. 'By jove, she's got it!'

Lizzy, dozing in her basket by the stove, lifted her head at Luke's excited tone, her tail thumping heavily on the floor.

'Have you, Martha?' Ruby asked.

I sat very still, forcing myself to think through it all logically, to make certain I wasn't simply grasping at straws because I was exhausted and injured. But no – the more I examined it, the more certain I became.

The motive was there. The means was there. The opportunity was there. And most tellingly, the character was there – the specific combination of desperation, capability, and moral conflict that would drive someone to murder while still leaving them wracked with guilt afterwards.

I thought about the attack on me, about Ruby's observation that it seemed almost restrained compared to Stan's calculated murder. That made perfect sense now. The murderer hadn't wanted to kill me – had perhaps even been horrified by the necessity of attacking me at all. But they'd been desperate to stop my investigation and prevent me from finding out the truth.

A truth I had now uncovered anyway.

'Yes.' I nodded. 'Yes, I have.'

'By George,' said Dr Briggs. 'How very marvellous.'

'What's next, Martha?' Maud asked.

'There's no time to lose,' I said. 'Vicar, can you fetch Ben from the cottage and ask that he bring Detective Inspector Kennington with him?'

I would ask Ben, and Detective Inspector Kennington, to gather everyone immediately before anyone had a chance to flee – all the suspects together in the Cricketer's Arms. I would lay out my case and force the murderer to confront what they'd done.

It would be dramatic, certainly. Perhaps even melodramatic. But it felt right somehow – a public revelation to match the public nature of Stan's death at the cricket match. There was a certain sort of irony in that.

14

Luke left immediately, his long strides carrying him quickly down the path. Dr Briggs followed at a more sedate pace, stopping at the gate to wave his farewell.

'May I know what you have planned?'

'I'm going to ask the police to gather everyone at the Cricketer's Arms,' I said.

'I think I should attend,' he said firmly. 'I may be needed.'

'Yes.' I nodded. 'I think that would be a very good idea.'

As soon as the door closed behind them, Ruby turned to me with wide eyes. 'Martha, are you absolutely certain?'

'I am, based on everything we've learned, and the evidence in front of us.' I stood, my legs feeling steadier than they had all day. 'Everything fits – the motive, the means, the opportunity, and most importantly, the character.'

'Who is it?' Maud demanded. 'Don't keep us in suspense, dear. We're not all as logically gifted as you are. I, for one, don't have the faintest idea who it is.'

I shook my head. 'I'd rather just go through everything once, if you don't mind. It would take too long to explain, and besides, it will only take Luke two minutes to get to the cottage. They will be back shortly.'

'Then do sit down and rest a moment, Martha,' Ruby said. 'You're acting very bravely but inside you must be terrified.'

'I am rather,' I admitted as I walked into the parlour and dropped into my favourite chair.

I closed my eyes and breathed deeply. No sooner did I feel myself relaxing than a knock on the door signalled the arrival of Ben and Detective Inspector Kennington.

'Martha?' Ben stood in the doorway of the parlour. 'Detective Inspector Kennington has some questions.'

'I most certainly do, Mrs Miller.' The other detective stared at me with open hostility, his voice overly loud in the small room. 'Starting with why you carried on an investigation when I told you to cease all interference in the case.'

'Perhaps you can save the admonishments until later?' I asked weakly. 'I'm recovering from a rather nasty head injury.'

'Well, yes, I understand that.' Thankfully, his voice was pitched at a more acceptable level. 'But that hasn't stopped you meddling, has it?'

I stared at him in what I hoped was a haughty confidence. 'Is it still meddling if I have solved your case for you?'

'That remains to be seen, doesn't it?'

'If I am wrong, then please, arrest me for wasting police time.'

'This is highly irregular.' He paced up and down, moustache twitching with disapproval, though he did seem a little calmer. 'In my experience, amateur sleuths often jump to premature conclusions.'

'Then consider this an opportunity to prove me wrong,' I said more sharply than I'd intended. The throbbing in my head was making me irritable. 'But, unfortunately, I'm certain that I'm not.'

Ben touched Kennington's arm. 'If I may interject? Mrs Miller has proven herself remarkably capable in previous investigations. I think we should allow her to present the case at the Cricketer's Arms. If at any point you think things are getting out of hand, we can both step in.'

Kennington regarded me for a long moment, his expression unreadable. Finally, he nodded. 'Very well. I understand the vicar has gone to the pub to speak with the publican. I shall gather the suspects there but, Mrs Miller, if this turns out to be some sort of parlour trick—'

'It won't be.' I met his gaze steadily. 'Someone in this village murdered my husband, then attacked me in my own garden. I can assure you that this is not a game to me.'

'Very well.' He looked down at his wristwatch. 'Shall we say seven o'clock? Will that give you time to prepare?'

'Yes, thank you,' I said, though I wondered what on earth he thought I had to prepare. I had notes I'd taken for my own use, but I didn't have a speech prepared. The case was in my head – I often didn't know what I was going to say until I said it.

Ruby saw the detectives out, and then came back into the parlour carrying my notes. 'I thought you might need these.'

'Thank you.' I smiled at her. 'It may help to have something to hold.'

As I took the handwritten pages from her, my hands trembled slightly – from nerves, tiredness, the head injury, or all three, I couldn't say.

'Martha,' Ruby said gently. 'You don't have to do this. You could simply tell Detective Inspector Kennington what you know and let him handle it.'

'No.' I shook my head, then immediately regretted the motion as pain flared behind my eyes. 'This person killed Stan and attacked me. It's important to me that I am the one to confront them. They need to face what they've done.'

Maud patted my shoulder. 'That's the spirit, dear. Now, shall we go down together?'

'Yes, let's.'

We walked to the Cricketer's Arms – Maud on one side and Ruby on the other. I had never felt both so afraid and so fearless at the same time. How could I possibly fail with these two at my side?

* * *

Maud pushed open the door to the pub and we stepped inside. The lounge had been arranged so chairs were placed in a rough semicircle facing a small table where Detective Inspector Kennington sat with a notebook open before him. Ben stood beside him, his expression grave.

My suspects, their friends and some family members sat in those chairs, watching me with varying degrees of curiosity, hostility, and apprehension. Winnie Noble, no doubt keen to make sure she didn't miss a thing, was rubbing at the bar with a dishcloth.

Oliver Beckwith sat with his injured ankle propped on a stool, his expression sardonic. Walter Preston lounged in his chair with studied casualness, but his eyes were hard. Bernard Harland looked exhausted, his face grey with strain. Ted Harland sat beside his brother, protective and suspicious. Lavinia Thompson perched on the edge of her seat, hands clasped in her lap, while Annie Raynor sat close beside her, radiating support.

Luke stood near the window, slightly apart from the others. When our eyes met, he gave me an encouraging nod.

'Mrs Miller,' Detective Inspector Kennington said formally. 'You've requested this gathering, and I have acquiesced. The floor is yours.'

Maud and Ruby walked over to stand with Luke, and I sat behind the table, next to the detective. I shuffled my notes, tried to ignore the ache in my head, and cleared my throat. I might have the most terrible headache, but my mind was clear.

'Thank you, Detective Inspector. Ladies and gentlemen, you are all here because one of you murdered my husband, Stanley Miller, during the cricket match on Saturday. Furthermore, that same person attacked me in my garden on Saturday evening, striking me with a tree branch and leaving me unconscious.'

A murmur rippled through the room, and Detective Inspector Kennington held up a hand for quiet. He cleared his throat and waited until all eyes were on him before he spoke. 'The pathologist has confirmed Dr Briggs' initial assessment of Mr Miller's death that he was killed by poison. At this stage, we do not yet have the test results back from the laboratory in Reading. However, all evidence points to the poison as being monkshood, and such poison was administered to Mr Miller as a paste which was placed into his cricket gloves.'

'Wicked,' Winnie Noble murmured from her place at the bar.

Detective Inspector Kennington shot her a withering look before continuing. 'The poison was absorbed through the skin of Mr Miller's palms, causing rapid cardiac arrest. He collapsed and died within minutes, but let me be clear: this was not a quick and painless death. It was swift, perhaps, but far from merciful. Over to Mrs Miller.'

I took a moment to compose myself before I spoke. Stan had died a horrible death and the murderer deserved to face justice for what they had done. He had left Westleham without a word but had shown his true character on his return. That was the version of Stan that I would choose to remember fondly.

'The murder required three things: motive, means, and opportunity. Let's examine each in turn.' I made slow eye contact with each suspect in turn. 'Motive – several people had reason to want Stan dead. Mr Beckwith, you had not paid money meant for my maintenance, and had a very public disagreement with Stan about it.

'Mr Preston, Stan was back in Westleham and determined to put right things he had done wrong in his life. He wanted you to come clean about your property dealings, which would have been financially damaging and publicly embarrassing.

'Mr Bernard Harland, Stan discovered illegalities connected to your business, and threatened to report you unless you stopped.

'Mr Edward Harland, you are exceedingly fond of your brother and would not have wanted shame brought upon your family because of your brother's activities and would have done anything to protect him.

'Lavinia, you were hurt by Stan's cruel dismissal of your past relationship, which you overheard.'

'What about you, and the vicar?' Winnie Noble called.

'Unless you think I hit myself over the head, I rather think I'm in the clear,' I said dryly. 'As for Mr Walker, let's examine the facts. On the morning of the game, the vicar was one of the first people on the cricket green. He was captain of the team and was in the middle of the field immediately prior to the game starting. I brought over Stan's cricket kit from the house. There was no opportunity for Mr Walker to touch that kit. Winteringham won the toss, and elected to field. That meant the vicar was first in to bat. As he remained not out, he was still on the field when Stan collapsed.

'In addition, the person who attacked me was a good deal shorter than the vicar who, at six feet tall, would be a rather imposing figure looming over me in the shadows before I was attacked.'

Winnie Noble made a disapproving noise in her throat, clearly displeased that Luke had been eliminated so quickly. I ignored her.

'Moving along to the second requirement: means. The murderer needed knowledge of poisons, access to monkshood, and the ability to prepare and apply a contact poison without being observed.' I turned to Bernard. 'Mr Harland, you have extensive pharmaceutical knowledge. You worked with a medical unit during the war. You know exactly how contact poisons work, how to prepare them, and what dosages would be lethal.'

Bernard nodded slowly. 'I do. But that knowledge is circumstantial. It doesn't prove I used it.'

'Quite right. You were a spectator at the cricket game and could have gone into the unlocked pavilion at any time to put the poison into Stan's gloves. You were also in the village at, or around, the time of the attack on me.'

'I've already told you I did not do that.' Bernard sounded quite desperate. I forced myself to ignore him and carry on.

'Mr Beckwith, you had motive but due to your injured ankle, it is very unlikely that you could've walked to the cricket ground aided by your stick, made your way into the pavilion with a deadly poison, administered it, and then made your way home without being seen. Additionally, there's no evidence to suggest you know anything about poisons, or deadly plants. Moreover, I cannot conceive of you being able to strike me with sufficient force to knock me unconscious. Why would you wield a tree branch, when you could've just hit me with your stick?'

Oliver inclined his head, accepting this logic.

'Mr Preston, you most definitely had the means: you had specifically asked for monkshood to be planted in your garden, and you were aware of its deadly qualities because you were told by your gardener, Frank Bennington, that it was dangerous. You were seen at approximately eleven o'clock in your garden smoking on the evening I was attacked. It wouldn't have taken long for you to come into the village and attack me. Finally, gardening gloves went missing from your shed. At first I thought whoever took the gloves was perhaps doing so in an attempt to frame you. Then I realised that might not be right. Whoever killed Stan would have needed gloves to handle the plant and make the poison. I learned nothing to suggest that person was you.

'Ted Harland,' I continued. 'You were fiercely protective of your brother. You might have killed Stan to prevent him from reporting Bernard's activities. However, you were the one who told me about Bernard's pharmaceutical knowledge and his presence in the corridor late Saturday night. If you killed Stan to protect Bernard, why would you draw attention to both your brother's capabilities and movements?'

Ted met my gaze steadily. 'I wouldn't.'

'Precisely. You've been trying to protect Bernard, certainly, but from unjust accusation, not from consequences of murder. I also accept that you were very fond of Stan.'

I took a deep breath. Only one suspect remained.

'Which brings us to Lavinia Thompson.'

Every eye in the room turned to the pale woman sitting beside Annie Raynor. Lavinia's hands were still clasped in her lap, but I could see them trembling.

'Miss Thompson, you were in a relationship with Stan, and I am told that you were devastated when it ended. So heartbroken, in fact, that you have not had another relationship since. You were even sitting in the bar of this very pub, hoping for a glimpse of him. Perhaps all those old feelings came back, and you hoped that somehow he would see your worth. But that did not happen. Instead you overheard thoughtless words said about you before the cricket match started. You then ran away, clearly distressed. What did you do then, Miss Thompson?'

'I—' She shook her head. 'I don't know what you mean.'

'What did you do after you left the cricket green?'

She paused again, and Annie gasped. 'Tell Mrs Miller where you went, Lavinia.'

'I didn't go anywhere,' she said as tears ran down her face. 'I didn't do anything.'

'You dye your own embroidery threads, don't you?'

'Yes.' She nodded. 'But I don't understand the relevance.'

'I assume you do that rather a lot.'

Lavinia's look of confusion mirrored everyone else's. 'Yes.'

'When I first met you, I noticed how neat and tidy your appearance was,' I said. 'Everything except your hands. It seemed strange to me that someone who was clearly as fastidious about their appearance as you are would have stained hands.'

'I can't help that.' She looked down at her hands, as though they had betrayed her, which, in a way, they had. 'It's the nature of dyes. I can't always get it all off my hands.'

'Someone who dyes threads often, as you admit to, would have extensive knowledge of plants and their properties. Anyone who works with plant dyes knows which plants are useful and which are deadly. You would certainly know about monkshood.'

'So I know about plants?' She shrugged. 'That doesn't prove anything.'

'I think you were so upset at Stan's words that you hatched a particularly evil plan. Perhaps you walked by the churchyard and saw the monkshood. Maybe you walked along the lane in the direction of the farm and saw it in Walter Preston's garden. Either way, you realised that after all these years, Stan had never returned your very deep feelings for him and perhaps that knowledge disturbed the balance of your mind and you did something that ordinarily you would never contemplate.'

'Oh, Lavinia,' Annie said. 'Please say that you didn't.'

'Then you lied to me,' I went on. 'When I asked you where you were on Saturday night you said you were in your room, but Miss Raynor had visited you and knew that you were not.'

'I told you where I was,' she protested. 'I was in the church.'

'What were you doing in the church?'

'Praying,' she whispered. 'I don't know why you're asking me that. I've already told you.'

'You asked me to forgive you.' Those words had seemed odd at the time, but I hadn't realised their importance until much later.

'For not telling you about the argument I overheard between Stan and Mr Bernard Harland!' Lavinia's face twisted in rage. 'You know that's what I meant.'

'I know that's what you said,' I told her quietly. 'But I don't believe you. I think that, in your own way, you were asking for forgiveness for what you had done. I don't know whether you really went to the church on Saturday night or not. Perhaps that was just a fabrication you made up for not being in your room when Annie called by to return your scissors. Or perhaps you really did go because you had committed a quite ghastly sin.'

'No.' She shook her head. 'It's not true.'

'Which part?' I asked calmly, then leaned forward and lifted my hair off my face and pointed to the wound on my head. 'That you didn't kill Stan, that you didn't do this to me, or that you didn't go to the church?'

She looked intently at me for a moment, then dropped her gaze. 'I didn't do it.'

'Lavinia,' I said quietly. 'I forgive you. I know what it is to deeply love someone that you cannot have.'

'You do not!' she raged. 'Stan didn't love you! He never loved you.'

'Lavinia.' Annie grabbed her friend's hands in an attempt to calm her down. 'Do stop shouting. You sound a little unhinged.'

'I know Stan didn't love me,' I told her. 'But he didn't love you either. And that's why you killed him, isn't it?'

For a long moment, she said nothing. Then, in a voice barely above a whisper, she began to speak.

'He humiliated me. Again.' The words came out in a rush, years of pain and resentment pouring forth. 'Before the war, he cast me aside without a second thought, and married you. I loved him, and he treated me like I was nothing. Like I was a nuisance to be rid of.'

She looked up at me, her eyes red and swollen. 'I never married. I never even looked at another man. I kept hoping – foolishly, stupidly hoping – that someday he would realise what he'd lost. That he would come back and tell me that he'd made a terrible mistake.'

'How did you feel when you saw him again?'

'I thought when he saw me that he would finally see me. He would realise that I had been faithful all these years, waiting for him.' She laughed bitterly. 'But instead, he treated me exactly as he had before. Worse, even. He spoke about me as if I were some pathetic creature he wished he'd never met.'

'So you decided to kill him?'

'I didn't plan it. Not at first.' She wiped her eyes with the back of her hand, smearing the tears across her cheeks. 'But suddenly all the love I'd had for him turned into this all-consuming rage and I could feel it bubbling inside me. I know it's a terrible cliché but something inside me just... snapped. I was humiliated and heartbroken again, and he was just going to get on with his life as if I'd never existed. As if my love had meant nothing. I couldn't bear it.'

'So you poisoned his cricket gloves?'

'I saw the monkshood in someone's garden, and the plan just came to me fully formed.' She glanced scathingly at Walter Preston. 'Who does that? Who keeps deadly plants in their flower beds?'

He shrugged carelessly. 'I liked the colour.'

His comment was exactly the sort of thing I had come to expect of him. I turned back to Lavinia. 'Then what happened?'

'I found gardening gloves in his shed. It was easy enough because everyone was so busy with the stupid cricket game. I must admit, I was a little worried when I went into the pavilion that I wouldn't know which things were Stan's, but I shouldn't have worried. All of his equipment was named.'

'And me?' I asked. 'What about me?'

'I was horrified when Stan died. Then I panicked.' Fresh tears spilled down her cheeks. 'I thought if I frightened you, you would stop asking questions. I didn't want to hurt you badly. I just wanted you to stop. I thought if I could just get back to Winteringham, I could pretend none of it had happened, and it was all a rather bad dream.'

Detective Inspector Kennington stepped forward. 'Lavinia Thompson, I'm arresting you for the murder of Stanley Miller and the assault of Martha Miller.'

As he recited the formal charges, Lavinia sat perfectly still, her tears falling silently. Annie, still sitting at her side, looked utterly dumbfounded.

As she was led towards the door, she looked back at me and her face crumpled. She stopped suddenly and turned back to me. 'I wasted years of my life loving someone who never existed. At least now it's over.'

* * *

Bernard and Ted Harland approached me together. 'We want you to know how grateful we are. You didn't reveal the extent of Bernard's activities, or his gambling, and for that we're extremely grateful.'

'I respected Stan,' Bernard said. 'He was helping me reform, trying to make me into a better man. I shall always be grateful to him for that. I promise you I will turn my life around. It's what Stan wanted me to do, and that's what I must do.'

'I believe you can do that,' I said. 'Good luck, Mr Harland.'

The brothers left, Ted's hand on Bernard's shoulder in a gesture of support that spoke of genuine love between them.

'Martha,' Ruby said softly. 'You were magnificent.'

'I was terrified,' I admitted. 'My hands are still shaking. I was so worried I wouldn't be able to get her to confess and, so far as I'm aware, there's absolutely no proof she did any of the things she just admitted to.'

'You can be certain we will search her room upstairs thoroughly,' Detective Inspector Kennington said grimly. 'I'm sure there will be something. She's hardly a criminal mastermind.'

Perhaps not, but she had eluded him.

'You should be very proud.' Maud patted my shoulder. 'You found Stan's killer and brought her to justice. Well done, Martha.'

'I don't feel proud. I feel sad.' I slumped into my chair. 'Lavinia wasted her entire life loving a man who never deserved her devotion. And in the end, that wasted life led to murder.'

'How did you work it out?' Ruby asked.

'Partly Luke's sermon,' I said. 'And partly Lavinia's own words, but it took time for me to put the two things together. She said she wanted him to suffer. We thought she meant in relation to the argument we overheard between him and Bernard. But I think, even then, she was almost telling me what she'd done.'

'Will she hang?' Ruby asked.

'That's for the court to decide,' Ben said gently. 'But given that it was a crime of passion and considering her previously good character, she may receive a lesser sentence.'

'She planned it,' I objected. 'It wasn't an accident, or a sudden loss of control, no matter what she says. There were a lot of steps for her to take between being angry at Stan and putting poison in his cricket gloves.'

'I don't disagree,' he said. 'Thankfully that isn't for us to decide.'

Detective Inspector Kennington approached as we prepared to leave. 'Mrs Miller, I must admit I was sceptical about your abilities. I was wrong. That was exemplary detective work.'

'Thank you, Detective Inspector,' I said. 'It's very kind of you to say so.'

'However,' he added sternly, 'I would appreciate it if in future you would bring your theories to the police rather than staging dramatic revelations.'

'I'll keep that in mind,' I said, though we both knew I was making no promises. After all, he had agreed to the 'dramatic revelation' as he now called it.

As we walked out of the pub, I hung back to talk to Luke – I knew he wouldn't come back to the house with us.

'Are you all right?' he asked softly.

'I don't know,' I admitted. 'I solved the case. I found Stan's killer. But I don't feel triumphant. I just feel... empty.'

'That's because, despite everything that was between you, you have still lost your husband. You also understand that Lavinia's crime came from pain, not evil. That doesn't excuse what she did, but it makes it harder to hate her for what she did.'

'She wasted her life on him, Luke. And in the end, it destroyed her.'

'Yes.' He was quiet for a moment. 'Martha, what she said about Stan – about him not loving you—'

'Oh, Luke, I've always known that. I think I even knew that on the day we got married.'

'I must ask you' – he paused as though not quite sure how to continue – 'now probably isn't the time, but I must know. When you said you understood because you loved someone deeply that you couldn't have, did you mean—'

'Of course I did,' I said, but still didn't say the words out loud. Luke was right. Now was definitely not the time.

'Yes,' he said and smiled at me, then seemed to realise that what he'd said hadn't made sense. 'Me too. Apart from the last bit. The part about not being able to have that person.'

I decided to change the direction of our conversation before it went any further. After all, we were standing outside the front of the Cricketer's Arms. For all I knew, Winnie Noble could be hanging out of an upstairs window pretending to polish the glass.

'Will it be strange for you to conduct Stan's funeral?'

'No,' he said immediately, and I knew that was the truth. 'I'll be carrying out a necessary, though sad, part of my job. Who that person was in life is not relevant. We are all the same before God, whether saint or sinner.'

'I should get home.' I indicated Maud, Ruby, and Ben who were waiting for me.

'Good night, Martha,' he whispered. 'Sleep well, my darling.'

Luke waved to the little group as he crossed the road and walked towards the vicarage. I could hardly believe that he had uttered those last two words to me.

I knew that I would treasure those words, just as I knew that the next few months would not be easy for us. Everything had changed with Stan's death, but equally some things had not changed. We still lived in a small village where opinions were strong and memories long, and where a proper period of mourning was expected – especially when a widow's affections lay with the village vicar.

15

Monday morning came after one of the most restful sleeps I'd had in months. It was Ruby's last week at work, and she would get married at the weekend. The cheque Oliver Beckwith gave me was sitting on my dressing table and reminded me that everything in my life was changing.

Even though Ruby was moving out and no longer paying board, I would not suffer financially. The cheque would take care of my modest needs for months.

Although I'd spoken to Ted and Bernard after Lavinia had been taken away, I felt that there were still things left to be said between me and the brothers.

I found them sitting on the bench near Oliver Beckwith's office, their packed bags at their feet.

'Good morning, Mrs Miller,' Ted called with a wave.

'All ready to go home?' I asked, even though it was perfectly obvious that they were. 'I wanted to catch you before you left. Yesterday was so frantic, there were a few matters I thought we should discuss.'

'Oh?' Ted quirked an eyebrow. Bernard looked wary.

'I wondered if we might exchange addresses?' I gave an awkward laugh. 'That is, if I might have your address. You know mine, of course.'

Ted's shoulders relaxed. 'It would be nice to keep in touch.'

'I would like to write and let you know when Stan's funeral is.'

'Oh.' Ted blinked. 'Oh, yes, I see. We would like that, wouldn't we, Bernard?'

'Yes,' his brother agreed. 'That's very thoughtful of you, Mrs Miller.'

'About Stan's things—' I began.

'I shall have everything packed up and sent on to you,' Ted said quickly.

I shook my head. 'That isn't what I was going to say. You already know ours was not a conventional marriage, so I hope you won't think I'm unfeeling when I say that I would be more than happy for you to keep any of Stan's things that you would like.'

'That's exceptionally generous,' Ted said quietly. 'I will, of course, send on his personal papers. You'll need those.'

'I think I shall need to engage a solicitor.'

'If I may be so bold,' Ted said with a wicked glint in his eye, 'perhaps choose someone different to Oliver Beckwith.'

I laughed. 'That's excellent advice.'

Ted returned my smile, though his eyes were sad. 'If you let me know the name and address of the firm you choose, I'll take care of that for you. The police have a few things, a bank book, and a couple of other personal items but obviously most of the paperwork in relation to his investments is at the house in Brighton.'

'Thank you.' I hesitated; this was such a strange situation to be in. 'I'm glad Stan had good friends. When he returned to Westleham, he looked happier than I'd ever seen him.'

Ted's eyes looked suspiciously bright. 'There's something I want you to know. About what Lavinia said—'

'Oh no,' I interrupted. 'Please, you don't need to contradict what she said. I've always known Stan didn't really love me.'

'Perhaps not,' Ted said, but his words were not unkind. 'But he did respect you. He was also very sorry for the way he treated you. He always said you were a good woman. I see now what he meant.'

I fished a handkerchief out of my handbag. 'Goodness.'

'Oh dear,' Ted said. 'I'm very sorry. I didn't mean to upset you.'

'It's been an extremely difficult few days.' I dabbed at my eyes. 'For all of us.'

'He wasn't a perfect man,' Ted said. 'But he was trying to be better. That counts for something, doesn't it?'

'It does,' I agreed. 'It counts for quite a lot, actually.'

We sat in silence for a moment, three people who'd shared part of our lives with Stan in different ways, each of us mourning him in our own way, and trying to make sense of his death.

I stood to leave, and Ted stood as well, offering his hand. I shook it, then Bernard's.

'Take care of yourselves,' I said. 'And, Ted – please keep Bernard on the straight and narrow. Stan would have wanted that.'

'I'll do my best.'

'Safe travels.'

Ted gave a brief nod, his mouth tightening as if he wanted to say more but couldn't find the words. I walked away feeling the weight of everything left unsaid pressing at my back as I stepped back into my life and left them to go back to theirs.

* * *

Friday evening, the night before the wedding, Ruby and I sat in the parlour with Ada Bennington, who had come to help with final preparations. Ruby's wedding dress hung on the wardrobe door – a beautiful cream silk that Ada had altered to fit perfectly.

None of us mentioned that it was the same dress that Ada had worn only a few months earlier. The war had changed a lot of things – the ability to buy new clothes for a wedding was one of them. Ruby could have used her clothing coupons but wisely she was saving those – she'd soon need new things. The dresses she favoured were not the sort that could be easily let out to accommodate an expanding girth.

'You're going to look absolutely stunning,' Ada said, adjusting the hem one last time. 'Ben won't know what hit him.'

Ruby blushed prettily. 'I just hope everything goes smoothly. I keep worrying something will go wrong.'

'Nothing will go wrong,' I assured her. 'We've checked everything twice. Mother and Father are at Village Edge. The flowers are ordered, the cake is ready, the church is prepared, and you have the perfect dress. What could possibly go wrong?'

'Don't say that!' Ruby exclaimed. 'You'll jinx it.'

Ada laughed. 'You're both being superstitious. It's going to be a lovely day.'

'Didn't we have enough excitement last week?' Maud asked. 'This weekend everything is going to be just perfect.'

'Have you quite recovered?' Ada asked. 'With all the wedding preparations I haven't stopped to ask how you are.'

'I'm all right. The headaches have more or less stopped now.'

Ada peered at my head. 'You can hardly tell you even had a bump.'

I smiled at Ruby. 'Ruby has been teaching me to style my hair so it covers the bruise. I'm just glad I wasn't seriously hurt. Though, of course, nothing would have made me miss this wedding. I'm so excited to see my little sister become a married woman.'

'I'm rather worried about that,' Ruby confessed. 'Being a wife is extremely grown up, isn't it?'

'Goodness me, what is there to worry about?' Maud asked. 'The only thing I was worried about when I married Mr Burnett was the wedding night and, let's be honest, dear, you've already had yours, haven't you?'

Ruby flushed crimson, her mouth opening and closing like a fairground goldfish.

'Talking of wedding nights,' Ada said.

'No,' Maud said. 'I don't think that we should. We're absolutely not that type of friends.'

'I wasn't going to talk about my wedding night,' Ada clarified. 'But I was going to share some news with you.'

'Go on,' I encouraged.

'It seems that Mr Bennington and me... that is to say John and I... or is it John and me?'

'Good heavens!' Maud shook her head. 'Please just say it.'

'We're having a baby,' Ada said. 'Dr Briggs confirmed it this morning.'

'Oh, that's wonderful,' I said. 'How are the children taking the news?'

'Shirley is extremely excited,' Ada confessed, then wrinkled her nose. 'The boys, on the other hand, are not as thrilled. Frank said he thought his father was a little old for new stock.'

'Oh, that's hilarious!' Ruby laughed until tears ran down her face. 'But how lovely for you. I'm so very pleased for you.'

'I never thought it would happen to me at my age,' Ada admitted. 'John—'

'All right.' Maud held up a hand. 'I think we've had enough of that sort of talk for one night.'

Ada tried, and failed, to wipe the grin from her face. 'I should be getting home. John said he doesn't want me walking home on my own in the dark.'

'Come on.' I got to my feet. 'I'm sure Lizzy would love a walk. We'll see you home.'

'I'll say goodnight,' Ruby said and kissed my cheek. 'I don't want to have bags under my eyes in my wedding photographs.'

I was excited for Ruby but I tried not to think what tomorrow would mean for me. Tomorrow Ruby would marry Ben Robertson and they would live in Village Edge cottage. The house would be mine alone again – truly mine, now that Stan was gone and would never return.

I thought about Lavinia Thompson, wasting her life on a man who'd never deserved her love. I thought about Stan, unable or unwilling to love anyone properly. I thought about the years I'd spent in a hollow marriage, pretending everything was fine.

And then I thought about Luke – kind, steadfast Luke, who'd been willing to give up everything for me. Who saw me not as Stan's wife or Ruby's sister or Martha the invisible village woman, but as myself.

The woman he called 'my darling', and I smiled so widely at my friends that I was afraid my eyes would water.

* * *

Saturday morning dawned clear and bright – perfect wedding weather. I woke early, my first thought being that today was Ruby's day, and everything needed to be perfect.

Ruby was already awake when I went to her room, sitting at

her dressing table in her nightgown, staring at her reflection with a mixture of excitement and terror.

'Having second thoughts?' I teased gently.

'No! Absolutely not. I just... what if I trip walking down the aisle? Or forget my vows? Or—'

'You won't trip, you won't forget, and even if something small goes wrong, it won't matter. Ben loves you. That's all that matters.'

She turned to face me, her eyes bright with unshed tears. 'I can't believe this is actually happening. A little over a year ago, I was living with Mother and Father, miserable and convinced I'd end up a spinster. And now...'

'Now you're marrying a wonderful man who adores you, and you're going to be deliriously happy.' I pulled her into a hug. 'Come on. Let's get you ready to be Mrs Robertson.'

The next few hours passed in a flurry of activity. Maud arrived early to help, followed by Ada Bennington and Mother. The kitchen filled with chattering voices and the scent of the flowers that had been delivered that morning.

Ruby's hair was styled, her make-up carefully applied. When she finally stepped into her wedding dress, we all fell silent.

She looked absolutely beautiful.

The cream silk fell in elegant lines, and Ada's alterations had made it fit perfectly. Ruby's blonde hair was swept up, with a few soft curls framing her face. A simple veil completed the picture.

'Oh, Ruby,' Maud breathed, eyes bright as though she was the mother of the bride. 'You're stunning.'

Ruby turned to me, her eyes anxious. 'Really? I look all right?'

'You'll do, love,' our mother said from her place on my sofa.

'You look breathtakingly beautiful,' I said effusively to make up for Mother's matter-of-factness. 'Ben is going to lose his ability to speak when he sees you.'

She laughed, a touch of her anxiety easing. 'Good. Thank you, Martha.'

I helped her with her bouquet – lily of the valley threaded through with blush sweet peas and a few early white roses, simple but elegant – and we prepared to leave for the church. Several village women had already gone ahead to ensure everything was ready.

The church was packed. It seemed the entire village had turned out for the wedding, which was hardly surprising. Ben Robertson was well liked, and Ruby had become a popular figure in Westleham over the past year.

Ben stood at the altar, his face transforming as he watched Ruby approach on our father's arm. I'd never seen him look so happy – or so nervous.

Luke conducted the ceremony with warmth and dignity, his rich voice filling the church as he spoke of love, commitment, and partnership. When he reached the part about 'if any person can show just cause why they may not be joined together', a ripple of nervous laughter went through the congregation. After everything Westleham had been through recently, even the traditional words took on new significance.

But no one objected. Ruby and Ben exchanged their vows clearly and confidently, their love evident in every word. When Luke pronounced them husband and wife and Ben kissed his bride, the church erupted in applause.

As the happy couple processed back down the aisle, I caught Luke's eye. He smiled at me, and I felt warmth spread through my chest.

The wedding breakfast was held at the Cricketer's Arms, which Winnie Noble had decorated beautifully with bunting and flowers. Long tables had been set up in the pub's garden, and the May sunshine made everything feel festive and bright.

I'd worried that the recent murder would cast a shadow over the celebration, but everyone seemed delighted to have something joyous to focus on. Even Detective Inspector Kennington had come, looking surprisingly relaxed in civilian clothes as he chatted with other guests.

The celebration continued into the early evening. There was dancing – Luke asked me to dance, and though it was perfectly proper given the occasion, I was intensely aware of his hand at my waist, the warmth of his palm against mine.

'Happy?' he murmured as we moved in time to the music.

'Very. Though I'll miss having Ruby in the house.'

'She's just along the street. You'll probably see more of her now than you did when she was at work all day.'

'You're right.' I looked up at him. 'Still, everything's changing.'

'Is that a bad thing?'

'Not necessarily,' I said honestly. 'It's just... a lot.'

The dance ended and we separated to mingle with other villagers. Winnie Noble cornered me near the refreshment table, her expression avid with curiosity.

'Such a lovely wedding, Mrs Miller. Though, of course, under the circumstances, some might think it should have been postponed.'

'I can't imagine why,' I said pleasantly. 'Stan was my husband, not Ruby's. Ruby barely knew Stan, and Ben had never met him. I certainly wouldn't want her happiness delayed on my account.'

'I saw you dancing with the vicar,' she said slyly.

I looked pointedly at the area where couples were dancing. 'And now he's dancing with my mother. It's perfectly acceptable to dance at a wedding.'

I escaped before she could pursue the conversation further,

though I knew her small-mindedness was a sign of things to come. Some people wouldn't be happy if I observed a ten-year period of mourning before I allowed Luke to court me.

Such maudlin thoughts were for another day. They were certainly not for Ruby's wedding day.

The day finally drew to a close and guests threw rice as Ruby and Ben walked down the street towards their new home. I stood watching until they disappeared from view, feeling a mixture of joy and melancholy.

I knew I wasn't going to be alone – not really. Maud would still be next door. Ada would be popping in regularly, as would Ruby herself. I would always have Lizzy, and there was the hope that the village vicar would drop by for a cup of tea with increasing regularity.

16

The brass plate on the door read H. C. Fenwick & Co., Solicitors and Commissioners for Oaths. The lettering was neat, a little worn, and suggested a firm that prized order over show. Inside, the office smelled faintly of beeswax polish and pipe tobacco. A clock ticked loudly in the corner of the waiting room.

I had chosen a firm of solicitors in Reading to administer Stan's estate. Having never had need of legal services before, I had taken advice from Dr Briggs, who assured me Fenwicks was one of the best firms in the whole county.

A tall, spare gentleman in his early sixties introduced himself as Horace Fenwick, junior partner. His silver hair was immaculate, his manners impeccable.

'Mrs Miller,' he said, extending a courteous hand, as he showed me into his office. 'Please – do sit down. I've received a letter and a packet of documents from a Mr Edward Harland, who I understand was a close friend of your late husband.'

'Yes,' I said. 'Stan stayed with Ted and his brother Bernard in Brighton.'

Fenwick settled behind his desk and pulled at a pink bow

that held a buff folder closed. 'Quite. Mr Harland forwarded a number of bank statements and investment papers. Before we go into detail, I should mention that no will has been located – neither among these papers nor with your husband's previous solicitor in Westleham.'

I closed my fingers tightly around my handbag. 'What happens next?'

'There are certain formalities we need to take care of,' Fenwick said gently. 'In such circumstances, the law is straightforward. As Mr Miller's lawful wife, you are his sole heir. Once probate is granted, the entirety of his estate passes to you.'

I sat very still – this was what I had expected, but it was still a little surreal to hear someone tell me I had inherited money. 'I see.'

He adjusted his spectacles and glanced again at the documents. 'You may wish to brace yourself, Mrs Miller. Your husband was evidently a shrewd man. His post-war investments – mainly reconstruction bonds and several private ventures – have prospered remarkably.'

'How interesting,' I said, hoping that's how I sounded. The things he spoke of meant nothing to me. People like me didn't have investments or bonds; they had a post office savings account.

He cleared his throat. 'The total value of the estate, allowing for tax and sundry deductions, stands at a little over thirty-seven thousand pounds.'

I blinked and cleared my throat. 'Thirty-seven—?'

'Thousand,' he repeated softly. 'A considerable fortune by any measure. I imagine your husband intended to see you comfortably provided for.'

For a moment I could only stare at the neat columns of figures that the solicitor presented for my perusal. All I could think of was what this would mean for my future. I'd give some money to my parents, of course. Some would go to Ruby and Ben, and the rest would provide a quite wonderful nest egg for years to come.

'I hardly know what to say,' I murmured.

Fenwick offered a faint smile. 'You needn't say anything just yet. We'll see to the formalities in due course. If I may give one piece of advice – make no hasty decisions. Wealth, like grief, takes a little time to comprehend.'

I managed a small, grateful smile. 'Thank you, Mr Fenwick. That's good advice. You can be sure that I will heed it.'

Our business was quickly concluded, and when I walked back onto the street, it somehow looked different to how it had when I'd gone into the solicitor's office.

Thirty-seven thousand pounds.

The figure repeated itself with the slow insistence of a church bell. It was an impossible sum to comprehend. How did one even go about spending such a vast sum?

In a daze, I wandered back to the station and waited for the train that would take me home. It was as though I was living someone else's life – someone much more fortunate than me.

As the train pulled into Westleham and the doors opened, an arm reached up to help me down onto the platform.

'So,' Luke said. 'Are you still talking to me?'

I frowned. 'Of course. What do you mean?'

'I thought perhaps if you were a lady of means now, you'd no longer want to waste your time talking to a penniless vicar,' he teased.

'If the penniless vicar is you, I shall always want to talk to you.'

'Seriously, though, Martha.' He caught hold of my arm and

looked down at me earnestly. 'I'll understand if you feel differently now. If things are not the same—'

'Do stop,' I said. 'Stan's money changes both nothing and everything.'

'How so?'

'It changes nothing between us,' I said quietly. 'But it has the potential to change our future. It gives us the ability to make choices we may never have contemplated.'

Now was not the time to make declarations and speak freely about our future, but I hoped he knew that day would soon come. It was only right that we observe a period of mourning for Stan before we could openly talk about our feelings and begin to make plans. Before Stan had come back to Westleham, neither of us had much hope for a future together. Now, and thanks in no small part to the legacy Stan had left for me, it would be very bright indeed.

'Such as?'

'Should we ever have need for a honeymoon, I think we might be able to stretch to two weeks in Bournemouth rather than the usual one.'

* * *

MORE FROM CATHERINE COLES

ACKNOWLEDGEMENTS

My heartfelt thanks to my wonderful editor, Emily, whose endless patience and gentle guidance make every story stronger.

To the wonderful team at Boldwood, for your enthusiasm, kindness, and professionalism – it's a joy to work with you.

To Alex Lee, whose narration brings my characters to life in the most fabulous way – your quiet competence and amazing talent makes it an absolute pleasure to work with you on every book.

To my dad, for ensuring every cricket reference was accurate – any mistakes that remain are entirely my own.

To The Abbey Murder Club (you know who you are), for your friendship, encouragement, and the occasional firm hand when my tendency to procrastinate takes over. Your belief in me has meant more than you know.

It's with the help of these people that every story (eventually) finds its way from the darkness of my doubts towards the light of publication!

ABOUT THE AUTHOR

Catherine Coles the daughter of a military father was born in Germany and lived most of the first 14 years of her life abroad. Catherine writes cosy mysteries that take place in the English countryside. Her extremely popular Tommy & Evelyn Christie mysteries are set in 1920s North Yorkshire. Catherine lives in northeast England with her two spoiled dogs who have no idea they are not human!

Download your exclusive bonus content from Catherine Coles here:

Visit Catherine's Website: https://catherinecoles.com

Follow Catherine on social media:

x.com/catherinecoles

facebook.com/CatherineColesAuthor

instagram.com/catherinecolesauthor

ALSO BY CATHERINE COLES

Poison at the Village Show

Daggers at the Country Fair

Death at Lovers' Leap

Murder on the Cricket Green

Printed in Dunstable, United Kingdom

81501242R00129